STEPBR(

A Hawthc

Book One

Also From Colleen Masters:

Stepbrother Billionaire by Colleen Masters

Stepbrother Untouchable by Colleen Masters

Damaged In-Law by Colleen Masters

Faster Harder (Take Me... #1) by Colleen Masters

Faster Deeper (Take Me... #2) by Colleen Masters

Faster Longer (Take Me... #3) by Colleen Masters

Faster Hotter (Take Me...#4) by Colleen Masters

Faster Dirtier (Take Me...#5) (A Team Ferrelli Novel) by
Colleen Masters

* * *

DEDICATION

To all my beautiful readers.

__Join thousands of our readers__ on the __exclusive Hearts mailing list__ to receive FREE copies of our new books!

__CLICK HERE TO JOIN NOW__

We will never spam you – Feel free to unsubscribe anytime!

Connect with Colleen Masters and other Hearts Collective authors online at:

__http://www.Hearts-Collective.com__,

__Facebook__, **__Twitter__**.

To keep in touch and for information on new releases!

STEPBROTHER BASTARD
A Hawthorne Brothers Novel
Book One

* * *

by Colleen Masters

CONTENTS

Prologue

Just Outside of Spokane, WA

The cool light of morning has barely begun to filter through the flimsy motel curtains, but my looming headache still throbs at this slightest hint of day. I can sense the impending hangover circling overhead like a sinister bird of prey, ready to dive down and ruin the rest of my day. It's not a sensation I'm accustomed to: I haven't had this much to drink since graduating college a few years ago. And now, I'm starting to remember *why*.

I pry open my eyes by a hair's breadth and groggily appraise my surroundings. The grubby motel room looks even bleaker in the cold light of day. But you get what you pay for, I guess—and this was the cheapest place I could find en route to my destination. Besides, I didn't need anything fancy last night. Just a place to crash before the second leg of my long drive from downtown Seattle to middle-of-nowhere Montana.

The former has been my home since finishing undergrad, the latter was my mother's, when she was a girl. My mom, Robin, has returned to her hometown of old for the summer, and summoned me and my two younger sisters to join her. She says she wants to get some painting done, fill her lungs with fresh air…but I can't help but wonder what else has motivated this return to her roots. Then again, I've never been able to suss out the rationale behind my mother's flights of fancy. Why should this time be any different?

Throwing off the scratchy, questionably clean comforter, I swing my legs over the side of the bed, gritting my teeth as the contents of my head throb painfully against my skull. Brushing my dark blonde, shoulder-skimming, and very disheveled hair out of my face, I scan the room for a coffee machine—caffeine is always my first order of any given day. My bleary eyes rove over my unopened suitcase, the singularly bad hotel art on the walls, and the trail of discarded clothing leading from the front door to the narrow bed I'm perched upon now…

All at once, the pounding in my head evaporates as my heart takes up the frenzied beat. The last twelve hours swim up in my boozy memory, walloping me with a series of realizations. First of all, for all the clothing scattered around the room, not a stitch of it happens to be on my body. Secondly, it isn't just *my* clothing that's strewn every which way—half of the items very clearly belong to a man. And as I whip around to peer over my shoulder in the dim half-light, I'm reminded of *which* man, in particular.

"Good lord…" I whisper, springing gingerly out of the motel bed. I clutch a sheet to my naked body, staring at the man I've been bunking with all night.

His face is turned away from me, but there's still plenty of him to see all the same.

Surprise gives way to amazement as I take in his broad shoulders, muscled arms, and heavily inked back. Faint red lines stand out among the numerous black tattoos—those are nail marks. *My* nail marks. I swallow a gasp as he rolls over to face me. He drapes one of those thickly corded arms across my side of the bed, as if reaching out for me. A tight twang of sensation pulses between my legs, and I become aware of the telltale, satisfied soreness there. While I rest my eyes on my bedmate's sculpted, slumbering face, the events of last night come back to me in a rush. As I recall the cause of that delicious soreness I'm feeling, my knees begin to quiver so hard that I can barely stand.

Pulling the sheet tightly around me, I dash into the motel bathroom and sink down heavily on the edge of the tub. I clasp my hand tightly over my mouth, trying to keep my jaw from smacking against the tile as it drops to the floor. But even so, a laugh of disbelief escapes from my throat. I know this was supposed to be a layover and all, but I didn't expect quite so much emphasis on the *laid* part.

Well, Maddie… I think to myself, letting out a deep sigh, you've *got a nasty hangover, a day-long drive, and a sexy stranger sleeping in your bed. What happens now?*

"Hell if I know," I mutter out loud, my baffled voice echoing off the grimy tiles of the motel bathroom. I've never been very good at embracing the unexpected. And waking up still-drunk next to a tatted-up bad boy on the way to a quiet family vacation is about the last thing I'd ever expect from myself.

What can I say? I've never been very good at half-measures, either.

Chapter One

The previous night

Seattle, WA

My best friend Alison McCain cocks her head at me, watching from the couch as I overstuff my suitcase for the coming two weeks. I've been multitasking—packing for my vacation while filling her in on the details of my latest breakup. Allie, on the other hand, is entirely single-minded, here.

"So wait," she says, gesticulating with her wine glass, "Did you break up with him, or did he break up with you?"

"It was mutual, Allie," I mutter, straining to zip up the seriously overpacked bag. This is a laughably typical predicament for me—I'm constantly over-planning, over-thinking, over-preparing. I've never managed to take even the shortest of trips without dragging half my earthly possessions along. On the one hand, this compulsive trouble-shooting makes me excellent at my job in event marketing, where something is always on the verge of going seriously wrong. On the other hand, it's obnoxious as hell, even to me.

"Maddie, Maddie…" my redheaded best friend sighs, taking a healthy swig of her Pinot Grigio, "It's never mutual. *Ever*. You were with this guy for six months. It couldn't have just evaporated like—"

"Fine," I sigh, leaning back on my heels. Allie is relentless in her dirt-digging. I may as well just hand over the buried treasure of my latest failed relationship and let her have at. "I was the one who wanted out, but I let Paul think it was a mutual decision."

"That sounds like the Madeleine Porter I know," Allie nods, sending her halo of short red curls bouncing, "I'm glad you finally pulled the plug. You guys have been on the fritz for…well…most of the time you've been together, actually."

"In more ways than you know," I reply, pulling myself up to fetch a glass of wine. If we're going to get into the nitty gritty of my love life, I'm going to need a drink.

"Do tell…?" Allie prods, swiveling around as I walk into the kitchen…or rather, the corner of my one-room studio apartment that's posing as the kitchen. I was lucky enough to get a job after graduating; plenty of my classmates didn't weather the post-recession market half as well. But at 24, I'm still not raking in enough dough to rent more than a couple hundred square feet. I tell myself it's romantic. Bohemian, even. But really…it's just my only option.

"Let's just say that things in the bedroom were…less than electric, there at the end," I tell Allie, pouring myself a deep glass of white wine.

"Really?" she asks, genuinely surprised. "But Paul is *gorgeous*. What I wouldn't do for cheekbones like his."

"One, your cheekbones are excellent," I inform her, flopping down on the couch beside her, "And two, he *was* gorgeous, and he'd be the first one to tell you."

"Ugh," Allie says, wrinkling her nose. "One of *those*."

"One of those, indeed," I reply, taking a sip of wine, "It's like, he expected me to get off on his well-manicured chest hair alone. I honestly think *he* could. And he certainly wasn't very forthcoming with any *other* methods of getting the job done…"

"Wait-wait-wait," Allie says, eyes widening into saucers, "Are you telling me he didn't take care of you? He seriously didn't even make you come?!"

"He almost did. Once…" I sigh, averting my eyes.

"But you were with him for a *six months*," Allie exclaims, "How in the name of all that is good have you survived without—?"

"I've been taking care of myself in that department, don't you worry," I assure her, "I mean, s*omeone* has to."

"Damn right," she says firmly, distress fading from her eyes. "Well, I'm proud of you for ending things with him, then. You deserve more than some rich, handsome, lawyer anyway."

"Isn't that the trifecta of excellence, where men are concerned?" I ask sarcastically, taking another long sip.

"For some women, maybe," Allie shrugs, "But not for you, Miss Porter. Not for you."

"Ugh. I know," I moan, letting my head fall back against the couch, "What is the matter with me? I tell myself that I should find a stable relationship, with a respectable, mature guy…"

"But then you get bored stiff by each and every one of them," Allie completes my thought, her vibrant green eyes sparking with insight. "Did it ever occur to you that you may be going after the wrong sort of guy?"

I cock an eyebrow at my best friend. Alison and I were roommates in college, long before we were both recruited by the same creative agency. And while I was holding down two uneventful long-term relationships over those four years, her dorm bed was a veritable revolving door for men of all stripes. And a few women, too.

"I'm just not as adventurous as you are, in that department," I tell her, "Not that I don't admire your inclusive attitude, but—"

"No one's saying you should go sow your wild oats all along the West Coast," she laughs, "But Christ, Maddie. You're in your twenties! If ever there's a time to be adventurous, it's now. You know what you are, my friend? You're a serial monogamist. And that wouldn't be an issue if it weren't also depressing the shit out of you."

I avert my eyes, a bit stung by her choice of words. The truth is, I *have* been depressed these past few years, but not because of my love life. I try not to dwell too much on the darker aspects of my life, but remaining positive takes constant effort. My struggle with depression began just as I was starting my last year of college, when my father was killed in a car accident. Collision with a drunk driver, who of course walked away unscathed. My dad, Archie Porter, wasn't just a father to me—he was my idol. My role model. Losing him was the worst thing that's ever happened to me. I'll be carrying the weight of it my entire life. Next to that pain, a breakup is nothing but a toothache. After all these years, I can usually make it through the day without getting mired down in that pain. But now that it's come to mind…

"I'm sorry, Maddie…" Allie says, her tone softening at once. "That was super insensitive of me. I know how much you've been through… But, isn't that all the more reason to look for what makes you happy, rather than playing it safe?"

"Sure. In theory…" I allow, shaking off the shadows in my mind.

"Maybe in practice, too," she smiles, draining her glass. "I know a really easy way you can start looking, too."

"Oh yeah?" I reply, "What's that? Pottery class? Meditation? Tinder?"

"Not quite," she begins, grinning conspiratorially, "These next couple of weeks, while you're on vacation, I want you to grant yourself one random hookup with a hot stranger."

I immediately choke on my wine, I'm laughing so hard. "Have you forgotten who you're talking to?" I splutter, "Your best friend, Maddie Better-Safe-Than-Sorry Porter."

"Really?" Allie replies, "I thought I was talking to Maddie Always-Up-For-A-Challenge Porter. What, do you need me to make this into a bet or something? Get that competitive streak of yours all fired up?"

"…No. You can't sway me *that* easily," I say, lying badly.

"Aha!" Allie crows, leaping to her feet and pointing a victorious finger at me, "Madeleine Abigail Porter, I bet that you can't bring yourself to have one random hookup by the time you come back from vacation. Are you gonna prove me wrong or what?"

"Dammit, Allie!" I groan, burying my face in my hands.

"I got you now!" she cackles, going to grab the bottle again. "Now you'll do it for sure."

"We'll see," I laugh, letting her pour me a second glass, "Which will win out, my hate of losing, or my hate of spontaneity?"

"The game is afoot," Allie grins.

I raise the replenished wine glass to my lips. What are the chances that I could *actually* throw caution to the wind and have some fun while visiting my family for two weeks? Breaking up with Paul sucked, to be sure, but we were hardly in love. My heart didn't take too much of a beating this time around. Probably, that's because I never really opened up to him. In the wake of Dad's death, I haven't really been able to feel much of anything—least of all passion. Maybe a little rebound would do me some good. But who the hell am I going to meet in the middle of the woods? I don't really dig the grizzled lumberjack type, myself. You never can tell what's hiding in those big, bushy beards…

"I'm gonna miss you at work while you're away," Allie goes on, tugging my train of thought onto another track. "It'll just be me, the Dragon Lady, and Mr. Intriguing finishing up the campaign while you're gone."

I chuckle at her cheeky descriptions of our agency's co-founders, Carol (the so-called Dragon Lady) and Brian (who insists on using the word "intriguing" at least twenty times a day, usually to describe the most mundane things imaginable).

"If it makes you feel any better, I'm not expecting the trip to be a laugh riot," I reply. "The Porter women don't do particularly well in enclosed spaces."

"Oof. I hadn't thought about that…" Allie says, "Which one are you worried about butting heads with this time?"

"Oh, just all of them. As usual," I reply with a wry laugh. While the shared grief of our father's passing brought us closer in some ways, the long-standing differences between me, my two sisters, and our mother have never ceased to cause trouble.

As long as I can remember, each of us Porter women has marched to her own distinctive beat. I was always the bookworm of the family, hoping to follow in my father's footsteps as an English professor. My middle sister, Sophia, always skewed a bit darker and more rebellious. Our baby sister, Annabel, is in some ways the most stable one of us all, though that makes her pragmatic and blunt, sometimes to a fault. But above all, it's our mother, Robin, who's always keeping us on our toes.

When my sisters and I were little, we fancied our mom to be some kind of fairy queen. We grew up in an old farmhouse in Vermont, just far enough away from Dad's university town to feel like another world; a world spun magic into magic by Mom's presence. She's always been stunning, with vibrant blonde hair and blue eyes with specks of gold—eyes my sisters and I all inherited from her. But while she was beautiful and imaginative, it always felt as though she was floating just out of our reach. And whenever one of us tried to pull her down from the clouds, she'd snap from good fairy to bad fairy in an instant. She'd become impatient and dismissive, as if she resented us for the responsibility we came along with.

Mom's a wonderful visual artist, a true maker, and her mind is always on the next inspiration, the next piece. She loved me and my little sisters dearly, but she preferred to nurture her works of art, rather than us. It was always our sturdy father we turned to for stability. He kept us all rooted to the ground while my mother drifted up, up and away; shoring up the moon and stars as we looked on with wonder. But since Dad has been gone, the rest of us have scattered to the wind.

And the thing is, I'm starting to think that we're actually better off that way.

"At least you have a new mission to distract you from all the family drama," Allie points out, wiggling her eyebrows suggestively.

"Yeah," I laugh, "Maybe I'll be thanking you for this little dare by the time I get back."

"We shall see," Allie says smugly, "We shall see. Hey, when are you shoving off?"

"As soon as this little wine buzz wears off," I tell her, "I really should have left right after work, but I wanted a little hang session with my best friend first."

"And I'm sure that has nothing to do with not wanting to spend a few extra hours with your family tonight, right?" she teases, nudging me playfully.

"Why, I have no idea what you're talking about," I say, widening my blue eyes with mock innocence.

"Sure. Right. I totally believe you," Allie laughs. "Well, I hope you'll at least try to have a good time. Maybe the whole thing will surprise you."

"Maybe..." I allow, "Though whenever my mother is involved, any surprises that crop up don't tend to be particularly good."

"Good ol' Robin," Allie says, shaking her head, "I can't wait to hear what shenanigans she's got cooked up for you out there."

"That makes exactly one of us," I reply, polishing off my wine.

After a bear hug and a reminder of my hookup-related marching orders, Allie hits the road. Now there's nothing standing between me and the impending family reunion besides eight hours of driving split up by one night in the cheapest motel I could find along the way. How's that for a luxurious getaway?

As soon as my buzz has faded, I steel my resolve, grab my gigantic suitcase, and bid adieu to my shoebox of an apartment. My iPod is loaded up with Florence and the Machine, Muse, and Bruno Mars. If I have to face the music, it may as well be the kind I can belt out on the highway.

Chapter Two

The aged, blue-haired motel receptionist looks at me skeptically as I do battle with my gigantic suitcase, trying to get the damn thing through the front door. Smiling through my embarrassment, I finally roll the behemoth up to the counter under her heavy-lidded gaze.

"Hi. I'm just checking in for the night," I tell her, "The name is Porter. Mad—"

"And how many of you are there?" she cuts me off, crossing her round arms.

"…Pardon?" I reply, taken aback.

"How many of your little friends are waiting out there to sneak in the second I turn my back?" she goes on huffily, "I wasn't born yesterday, you know. I know how you young people try to take advantage, sneaking around when my back is turned. We charge by the person, not just by the room—"

"Um. It's just me staying here tonight," I tell her evenly, choosing not to be offended by her assumptions.

"Uh-huh," she drawls, unconvinced.

"Ma'am, I'm really just stopping here to sleep," I press.

"And what's a sixteen-year-old girl doing on her own. In a place like this. At midnight. With a suitcase full of god knows what?" she asks, narrowing her eyes. "Answer me *that*."

Ah ha. That's what's going on here. By now, I should be used to it. Despite the fact that I'm 24, my 5' 3" height and petite figure tend to give people the impression that I'm a teenager. Most of the time, I'm mistaken for the youngest Porter sister, rather than the oldest. But hey, I'm sure I'll get a kick out of that someday. Without another word, I take out my driver's license and slide it against the sticky counter.

"This should put your mind at ease," I say briskly, "And as for the suitcase, well, I'm afraid I'm just something of a compulsive over-packer."

The would-be gatekeeper inspects my ID, peering through thick bifocals. At last, she seems to be satisfied that I'm not going to be throwing a keg party in my motel room. Or hiding a keg in my luggage, at that. But she's not quite done with the third degree yet.

"There won't be any *men* stopping here to meet you, right?" she asks, giving me a not-too-subtle once over. "Please tell me you're not *that* kind of girl."

I can feel my blood rising to a low boil. If there's one thing I have no patience for, it's shaming women on the grounds of their sexuality. My mother may be spacier than Sputnik, but she taught my sisters and me to be fiercely feminist in our thinking. I believe that every woman should have the freedom to make her own choices about her body, whatever those choices happen to be.

"Tell you what," I say to the woman behind the desk, "Let's just say that I'm the kind of girl who would like the key to her motel room now, please. Unless you'd rather I find somewhere else to spend my money tonight."

"Ugh. Fine," she says hurriedly, thrusting a square of scuffed plastic my way, "Have a lovely evening, *Miss*."

I grab my key and do my best to make a dignified exit, onerous baggage be damned. My room is on the ground floor of the split level motel, overlooking a leaf-clotted swimming pool and a stretch of highway. In one direction lies Spokane, Washington; in the other, Montana. I've still got half a day's drive before I reach my destination, a lake house my mother's rented for the summer in her old hometown. At least, she described it as a lake house when we talked on the phone. For all I know, it's actually a yurt. And come to think of it, she never mentioned renting specifically…we could very well just be squatting. You never can tell with Robin Porter.

Nudging the door open with my shoulder, I trundle into my darkened room. I decide not to inspect the space too closely—ignorance is bliss. After a cursory sweep for cigarette butts, condom wrappers, or dead bodies, I flop down onto the bed and gaze up at the water stains that blossom across the ceiling.

Though it's nearly midnight after a long day of work, suddenly I'm feeling wide awake. This isn't exactly a penthouse suite, but it's the first night I've spent away from my Seattle studio apartment in over a year. I've been working my butt off on the job—trying my best to impress Carol and Brian. Their creative agency, ReImaged, is a pretty small outfit, but we still have our share of huge clients. Though we offer a full range of services, we specialize in event marketing—planning parties and functions that double as interactive advertising for the company at hand. Allie and I have become the dynamic duo of the ReImaged event planning department. I love the variety and excitement that are built into my work, but it's easy to get swallowed up by a fast-paced job like mine. This vacation is a very rare occurrence, and even now I'm finding it hard to stop thinking about the tasks that are waiting for me back at the office. The second I get back, we're moving onto our next big campaign for the denim company Asphalt. I'm already chomping at the bit to get started.

It's going to be a struggle to stay in the moment during this little getaway. Maybe I should listen to Allie and make the most of it. But what am I going to do for fun here, raid the vending machines and watch porn by myself? Not really my idea of a good time. Don't get me wrong, I can appreciate a good dirty video as much as the next person—but falling asleep to Pay Per View, Point Of View in a crappy motel would just be *too* depressing.

As I stare up at the ceiling, a sudden dash of color catches my eye. The glowing shadow falls through the window above my bed, blinking softly in the darkness. Pulling myself to kneeling, I tug open the creaky venetian blinds to investigate. I don't have to look very far to find the source of the bright light. There, on the next lot over from the motel, is a low brick building facing the highway. The place was totally hidden from view as I drove up. It would be a fairly nondescript structure, were it not for the glaring neon sign blinking above it, luring in weary travelers like moths to a flame. The sign's directive is simple: "Drink Here" it reads, with an arrow pointing straight to the front door.

"Can't very well ignore a *literal* sign," I murmur, smiling at the kitschy signage. Maybe a nightcap would help me chill out?

The anxiety-ridden part of my brain reels against the suggestion, and I immediately question the wisdom of braving a dive bar on the side of the road…at midnight, by myself. But to my surprise, the long-dormant curious side of me insists on an adventure before turning in. I've had a lot of trouble getting excited about anything since Dad passed away. Even this slightest spark of interest is out of the ordinary. I can't just let it fizzle out.

Squaring my shoulders, I rise to my feet and suit up. And by suit up, I mean making sure that my canister of pepper spray is tucked handily in my back pocket. (Hey, you never know.) I don't want to wrestle with my suitcase again, so my current uniform of boyfriend jeans and a white tank top will have to do. I run my fingers through my long, dirty blonde bob, dash on some mascara, and head out into the warm June night.

Gravel crunches beneath my feet as I try and look casual, strolling toward the roadside bar. There are a couple of cars parked outside, and a handful of motorcycles to boot. I have about as much experience hanging around with biker types as I do kicking back with Siberian tigers. For all I know, they're equally dangerous company to keep. The men I've dated have always been upstanding, clean-shaven, law-abiding blokes...each one more painfully boring than the next. I've never been one to tangle with bad boys. But tonight, I'll wander into the tiger's cage. Even if only to see one up close.

With a deep, steadying breath, I step up to the door of the bar. I can hear voices and music from inside, an appealing sort of din. The wide front windows could use a good scrubbing, but I don't spot any bullet holes. That's a good sign, right? Wrangling my face into a neutral expression, I push open the heavy door and cross the threshold.

The signature smell of liquor, cigarette smoke, and sawdust rolls over me as my eyes adjust to the low light of the bar. An ancient juke box wheezes out a classic hard rock tune, which underscores the rumbling tones of male conversation. A group of men in leather cuts are huddled around the pool table in back, in the middle of a game. There are a few women hanging around them, too, rocking micro-mini skirts and bare midriffs. The bar itself, a long slab of rough hewn wood, is spotted with solo men, cradling their beers in silence and watching a hockey game playing on the TV hanging in the corner. There are enough people around to put me at ease, but not so many as to be overwhelming.

So far, so good. Now maybe I'll actually be able to relax and enjoy this drink. I sidle up to an empty stool at the very end of the bar and climb up. This place is definitely built for big, strapping men, so it actually does feel like a climb for my shorter self. The guys around me are so engrossed in their games and pints, that they don't even notice my presence. I have to admit, I'm just the slightest bit put out by this. I half expected all their heads to turn in unison when a new woman walked into their midst, like in the movies. Guess I'm not exactly what you'd call a classic head-turner, though honestly I don't spend too much time worrying about it.

I peer around the stoic, handlebar mustachioed man sitting one stool down for me, searching for a bartender. As I run my eyes along the long rows of amber bottles and stacked glasses, a towering figure shifts at the edge my periphery. I swing my blue-eyed gaze toward the end of the bar and find that a tall, broad-shouldered man has appeared there. He stands facing away from me, his muscled back rippling beneath a plain black tee shirt as he reaches into the bar's cooler for a bottle of beer. His well-worn jeans are cut perfectly to his tapered waist, and I can't keep my eyes from taking a good, long look at his fine, sculpted ass.

But it's not until he turns my way that I feel the rest of the world fall away.

A crown of loose brown curls tumbles across his forehead, falling to just above his collar. Long enough to be gorgeously scruffy, but definitely not unkempt. His solid jawline is shadowed with dark stubble, giving way to sharp cheekbones and a full, firm mouth that's twisted into a wry half-smile. He's got to be over six feet tall, with a perfectly balanced and seamlessly muscled body; a body that strikes me as evidence of both a genetic miracle and a ruggedly physical lifestyle. But while this man would catch my eye any time he entered a room, it's his eyes that keep me staring at him with rapt, awestruck attention.

They're the most beguiling, brilliant shade of hazel I've ever seen in real life. Their color seems to shift with every move he makes. Yet it's the content of his eyes that's most arresting of all. There's a depth to his gaze that's seemingly bottomless. He has the eyes of someone who has seen worse things than most people can imagine, lived through harder times than many could survive. But despite that vast experience, there's mirth there too. The devil-may-care defiance of a true adventurer. Those right there are the eyes of a warrior. A knight. A man who's well acquainted with battle.

And right now, those eyes are swinging my way.

His gaze locks onto mine with a sniper's precision, and I watch as that small smile widens just a hair…at my expense.

"You must be lost," he says in a rich, clear baritone.

"Wh-what's that?" I stammer, feeling about two feet tall.

"I know every face that walks through that door," he goes on, nodding toward the exit. "And yours ain't one of 'em."

"Oh," I reply, straightening my spine, "I'm just, uh…passing through."

Passing through? I chide myself. *What is this, a John Wayne movie?*

The man behind the bar nods, amused, and begins to turn away without comment. I feel heat rise into my cheeks at being brushed off. What, is he just going to completely ignore me? I have as much right to be here as anyone else, even if I'm not exactly his preferred clientele. It's not exactly unreasonable to expect a bartender to take your drink order, is it? I call after him, trying to keep the annoyance out of my voice.

"Could I get a drink, please?" I ask him.

His head snaps back toward me with a look of indignation. He cocks an eyebrow, giving me a raking once-over that leaves trails of heat all along my skin. A searing pang twists my core—it feels something like longing. Or ire. Or both?

"Do I look like a fucking bartender to you?" the man shoots back at me, drawing the attention of a few other guys along the bar.

"Well…You do seem to be tending the bar," I point out, gripping the edge of my stool to keep my hands from shaking.

He tosses back his head, giving his dark curls a toss as he lets out a bark of laughter. In one swift motion, he sets the lip of his bottle against the bar and brings his fist slamming down, sending the cap flying.

"Nah. I'm just in a habit of getting what I want for my own damn self," he tells me, taking a long swig of beer. I watch those full lips press up against the glass bottle and feel a jolt of sensation run down my spine. He lowers the beer and shoots me an arrogant wink, "Don't jump to conclusions, babe."

"Don't call me babe, asshole," I shoot back before I can stop myself.

That gets his attention. For the first time, he actually seems to pause and consider me. That pang in my belly rings out to the very edges of my body as his gaze lingers on me. How can I be so viscerally attracted, so automatically responsive to someone who's clearly an arrogant dick? Maybe it's just pent-up sexual energy from these past few months of lackluster lovemaking with Paul... Though I suspect this new guy would have the same effect on me no matter when he happened to cross my path.

Those firm lips of his part, locked and loaded with a scathing comeback, no doubt. But before he can utter a syllable, an older voice rings out behind him.

"Hawthorne!" shouts a graying, barrel-chested man marching toward the bar from the stock room. "What part of 'wait to be served' don't you understand?"

"Don't know what to tell you, Jimmy," my sparring partner shrugs, knocking back his beer, "I'm not real good at taking orders."

"No, that's my job," grumbles Jimmy, taking his rightful place behind the bar. He catches sight of me sitting there and goes on, "Speaking of, what'll you have, sweetheart?"

I spot the dark-haired man watching me out of the corner of his eye. His very gaze feels like a challenge. A dare. And as usual, I find myself unable to pass it up. Normally, my drink is a mojito. But I have a feeling that wouldn't go over to well, here.

"Bourbon. Neat," I tell the bartender, whose eyebrows raise at my order.

"OK. Coming right up," he replies, turning away.

The tall stranger leans against the rough wooden bar, nursing his beer. He smiles at me with more amusement than kindness.

"Bourbon, huh? Was that for my benefit?" he asks condescendingly.

"Oh, absolutely," I drawl back, my words dripping with sarcasm. "I'm *very* invested in impressing you."

"I tend to have that effect on people," he replies nonchalantly. I try not to notice the way his built arms flex as he brings the beer to his lips. There's not an ounce of fat on that body of his—just muscle, sinew, and tons of ink. He's rocking a full sleeve of tattoos on his right arm. I find myself wondering where else he's tatted-up. Wanting to find out for myself...

"Here you go," Jimmy says, setting a lowball glass on the bar before me. Not exactly a light pour, either. But it's not like I can back down now.

I take the glass in my hand—the strong, smoky smell of the booze threatening to singe my eyebrows right off my face. The arrogant stranger's hazel eyes are hard on my face, his lips twisted into a rakish grin. But now that I'm feeling rightly competitive, I'm dead set on wiping that smug look off his face. Bracing myself, I bring the whiskey to my lips and knock back a long swig—half the glass at least. The powerful burn hits me like a sledgehammer at first, but then that satisfying, fiery buzz warms me all over. I have to say, I get the appeal.

Smiling triumphantly, I look up to watch the stranger's reaction…but no one's there. He's already fallen into conversation with another regular at the back of the bar, having totally lost interest in me. I'm far more disappointed than makes any rational sense. What do I care about holding the attention of some guy at a bar? Some intriguing, sexy guy I can't stop stealing glances at no matter how hard I try…

"Pull yourself together, Porter," I mutter under my breath, settling down to sip my whiskey and lick my wounds. Maybe I'm out of flirting practice after an entire young adulthood of monogamy. Though, come to think of it, I don't think I was ever *in* the practice of flirting to begin with. This whole random hookup challenge of Allie's might be a bit harder to complete than I thought.

"Well look at you, drinking all by your lonesome," a grainy, sneering voice says from over my shoulder.

The sudden address startles me, and I turn quickly around on my stool, guard raised. One of the biker guys has wandered over from the pool table to chat me up. His body looks solid as a tank, all bulging veins and flushed red skin. Thick dark hair covers his chest and arms, and I can't help but picture a gorilla pickup artist as I take him in.

"That's right," I inform him, trying to toe the line between ignoring and encouraging him. I pray that he'll take the hint and back off...but instead he steps up to the bar beside me, popping my bubble of personal space like it's his God-given right.

"I can fix that for you," he grins, booze thick on his breath as he leers at me, "Let me buy you a drink, Hun."

"Well, you know what they say," I reply coolly, "If it ain't broke..."

"Damn, girl! You've got some mouth on you," he laughs meanly, taking a long swig from his beer can.

"I'd love to know what else that mouth is good for, 'sides backtalk."

"Children talk back," I tell him, my face stony, "Women choose not to engage in conversation with men who make them uncomfortable."

"Is *that* what I'm doing? Making you uncomfortable?" the guy presses, leaning in close to my face. A cold spike of fear cuts through my annoyance with him. And that spike only drives in deeper as I see one of his buddies—a haggard, rangy guy—peel away from the group around the pool table and head our way. If they start something with me, I'm on my own to stop them. The owner, Jimmy, is down at the other end of the bar, eyes fixed on the hockey game. And who knows if I could even count on him, or *any* of the men in here, to stand up for a random woman over another local?

"Look. I'm just trying to enjoy my drink in peace," I inform the first man, as his buddy steps up to box me in. "Please respect that and leave me alone."

"Or what?" the hairy ape grins, crushing his beer can against the bar. "What the hell are you gonna do about it?"

"You need to work on your manners, Missy," the second man adds, cracking his yellowed teeth into a malicious grin. "Around here, it's up to you ladies to show us men some respect… Or at least a good time, if you catch my drift."

My hand inches toward my back pocket as they go on. I've never had to use my pepper spray on anyone before, but these guys are pushing me way out of my comfort zone. My mind spins desperately through the options at hand. Should I bolt? Stand my ground? Mace the shit out of these assholes?

"What do you say?" the first man grins, placing his hand dangerously low on the small of my back. "You gonna be a good girl and pay your respects?"

Fight wins out over flight for control of my body. I leap up from my stool and whip around to face the man who's harassing me, fingers closing around my canister of pepper spray. But the surge of adrenaline is shot through with baffled surprise as I watch a firm hand fall on the hairy man's shoulder and yank him away from me.

"The fuck do you think you're doing, Vaughn?" snarls the dark-haired Adonis who blew me off not ten minutes ago. His eyes are bright with contempt for the man he's pulled away from me, for reasons that still remain unclear.

"I'm just having a word with this lady, here," the man called Vaughn says defensively.

"Really?" says my unexpected defender, "Cause it looked like you were being a damned idiot and giving her a hard time."

"What the hell do you care?" Vaughn whines, "She's fair game."

"Fair game?" I echo, my voice dripping with ire, "What the hell is this, some kind of frat house? What grown man talks that way?"

"Couldn't have said it better myself," says my sudden ally, giving Vaughn a shove back in the direction of his biker buddies. I'm relieved to see that none of them rush to their friend's defense. Maybe this is a familiar routine with this jerk.

"You think you're noble or some shit, Hawthorne?" my aggressor grumbles, retreating with his grimy pal in tow.

"Not really," the hazel-eyed stranger replies, "I'm just not the kind of guy who enjoys picking on little girls."

My relief at being saved from those assholes deflates slightly. Is that how this guy sees me, as a little girl? Is that why he stepped in to protect me—because I don't look like someone who can stand up for myself? I'll own the fact that I was scared shitless for a second there, but still, I would have come out swinging if I'd had to.

"You didn't have to do that," I say, crossing my arms tightly over my chest. I'm suddenly very aware that my black bra is showing slightly through my white tank. "I could have handled those guys myself."

"Oh, is that so?" he grins back, peering down at me with those dazzling hazel eyes. "What exactly was your plan of action, huh?" I produce my canister of pepper spray for his appraisal, which only makes his patronizing grin grow wider. "Got a sidearm, huh? You're tougher than you look."

"And how tough do I look to you, exactly?" I reply heatedly.

"Not tough enough to be in a place like this on your own," he says frankly.

"Well, maybe I should get out of here then," I say, reaching for my whiskey and taking another big gulp that drains the glass. I have to say, I don't totally hate that burn after all.

"Why? You're not on your own anymore," he replies, settling onto the next barstool and giving mine a pat. "Now that you've got me for company."

"Did I say I wanted your company?" I shoot back, though of course I do.

"No. But I want yours," he replies evenly, taking my hand in his. Electricity shoots up my entire arm, shocking me into stillness. "And I'm in the habit of getting what I want. Remember?"

If anyone else in the world tried a line like that on me, I'd laugh in his face and walk away. But coming from this guy, it doesn't come off as bravado. Actually, it somehow has the ring of a promise to it. Maybe it's because he stopped those guys from harassing me, maybe it's his winning smile, maybe it's just the bourbon, but I do want to stay here and get to know him. At least a little. Every cell in my body is screaming to be closer to him, even if it's just as close as the next barstool.

"What's your name?" I ask him quietly, letting my hand rest in his.

"Cash Hawthorne," he replies, his fingers tightening ever so slightly around mine in something between a handshake and a caress.

"I'm Madeleine. Maddie," I tell him, pulling my hand away as the sensation finally becomes too much to bear.

"Well Maddie," Cash grins, "You just became my new drinking buddy for the night. I suggest you get comfortable. We're gonna be here for a while."

He catches Jimmy's eye and holds up a couple fingers. In a moment, two fresh glasses of bourbon have appeared on the bar before us. I settle down before my replenished glass, already very much feeling the buzz. I don't usually take my liquor straight, and though I'm no light weight, I have no doubt that Cash here could drink three of me under the table. But I know full well that there's no leaving now. Something about this guy has snagged my interest—and I intend to find out what that something is.

"To new friends," I say, lifting my glass to his.

"I'll drink to that," Cash says, knocking the rim of his glass against mine as those hazel eyes bore into me.

A new song comes on the jukebox as we sample our fresh drinks—it's "A Boy Named Sue" by Johnny Cash. The coincidence isn't lost on me.

"Wait a minute," I say, angling my body toward my sexy new companion. "You're not named after—"

"I am, as a matter of fact," he says proudly, "My dad is a big fan. All me and my brothers listened to growing up was Johnny Cash, CCR, and The Stones. Could have been worse though, right? What if he'd been into Hootie and the Blowfish?"

"That…would have been unfortunate," I laugh, feeling my guard lowering with every passing second. This guy is dead sexy *and* has a sense of humor? He's earning some checks in the plus column after a rather unimpressive start, that's for sure.

"Damn right, it would have been unfortunate," Cash says, his deep, changeable eyes lingering on me, "How in the hell would I get a pretty girl like you to have a drink with me with a name like Hootie?"

So he thinks I'm pretty. That shouldn't make me as giddy as it does. And yet…

"That interception you ran with those assholes still would have done the trick," I reply, "Thank you for that, by the way. I would have dealt with it somehow, but I appreciate you stepping in back there."

"Don't mention it," he shrugs, "Their bark is worse than their bite. Just a bunch of wannabe MC tough guys who watched a little too much *Sons of Anarchy*. Besides, they don't fuck with guys like me."

"Guys like you?" I ask, taking another sip of whiskey.

"Vets," he replies, putting away some more bourbon of his own.

"You're in the Army?" I ask, surprised. "But you can't be much older than me."

"I'm 26," he tells me, a hint of hardness coming into his voice. "Plenty old enough to serve. Hell, I was right out of high school when I enlisted."

"I guess so," I reply. It's so hard to think of guys that young fighting overseas. But then, there's nothing easy about that kind of life. "But I thought you said you weren't very good at taking orders?" I go on.

"I'm not," he replies bluntly, polishing off his drink. "There's a reason I'm sitting here with you instead of coughing up sand in some fucking desert right now."

"Oh. You're not, uh, serving anymore?" I ask haltingly, trying to keep up with the pace of his drinking out of nervousness. I've never actually known anyone in the armed forces, at least not well. Both sides of my family have always tended toward artistic and academic pursuits, not exactly compatible with military service.

"No, I'm not," Cash tells me, flagging Jimmy down again and signaling for another round. I hurry and drain my glass, wondering at the speed with which he changes the subject. Maybe his military record has something to do with that gravity in his gaze.

"And what about you?" he asks as Jimmy refills our glasses, "What's your story?"

"Oh. I'm. Uh. In marketing," I reply vaguely. It sounds pretty unimpressive, set next to active military service.

"Sounds fucking boring," he laughs, instantly dashing any tension between us… Negative tension, that is. There's still plenty of *another* kind of tension buzzing in the air around our bodies. I have to laugh along with him. He's not wrong.

"I promise it's cooler than it sounds," I say, palming my new glass. "I basically just throw awesome parties for rich companies and get paid for it."

I notice that his body has edged a bit closer to mine. I can feel the heat coming off his skin, radiating against me. What would it be like to feel that warmth everywhere? To be encompassed by him. Swallowed up…

"That does sound cooler. For a city girl like you, that is," he grins, snapping my attention back to the present. "I'm not sure I'd be any good at it."

"City girl?!" I exclaim, giving him a playful shove…which may or may not just be an excuse to lay my hands on that rock hard bicep of his. My fingers come away practically aching for more.

"Well, aren't you?" he shoots back, letting his arm rest casually on the back of my bar stool. I can feel myself getting more intoxicated by the second with the closeness of him. That plus the whiskey has me feeling more awake, more engaged than I have in…years. With a man, at least. And that's counting the months-long relationship I just got out of. I can barely even conjure up an image of Paul, with this guy sitting in front of me. He's like an eclipse, blocking out everything but himself in my eyes.

"I mean, I'm technically a city girl. Presently," I smile at him, "I've been living in Seattle since I finished college. But I grew up with my family in Vermont."

"A city girl *and* a dirty hippie then," Cash says, shaking his head, "Man, I sure know how to pick 'em."

"You've picked me, huh?" I reply, my voice dipping low in my chest. "Picked me for what, exactly?"

Cash's eyes flick up to meet mine before traveling down along the length of my body. "From the way you're talking," he says, his own voice going ragged around the edges with something that sounds a whole lot like want, "It sounds like you've already got something in mind for us."

"What, me?" I say with a grin, "I thought I was just a sweet little girl."

"I thought so too," he says, letting his fingers trail down my arm, "But I'm not afraid to admit when I get it wrong."

A long, charged moment unfolds between us, and my eyes flick down to his full lips. My head is swimming with wanting to taste him, but I can't tell whether he's going to kiss me or not. Finally, the pressure gets to me, and I break away to drain the rest of my glass.

"How about a couple beers?" I suggest.

"Sounds good to me," Cash says, slipping an arm around my waist. "Real good."

Cash and I go on talking into the night, letting our conversation wander wherever it likes. He tells me about the motorcycle repair shop he owns nearby, the boxing gym he frequents in his free time, his love of MMA and UFC. I, in turn, tell him more about the outrageous events I've produced for work, my love of good coffee and literature, my inextinguishable hiking habit that's only grown stronger since moving to the Pacific Northwest.

We're like two old friends who haven't seen each other in years. Well, two old friends who also would quite like to jump each others' bones, that is. At least, that's the vibe I'm getting from him. Could I be wrong? I've never been very good at telling whether a guy is interested in me or not. I usually need someone—i.e. Allie—to tell me when a dude is into me. I'm just in the middle of a story about me and Allie in college when my loose tongue gets the better of me.

"We were actually just hanging out earlier, me and Allie," I tell Cash, my knee brushing up against his as we commune over our beers, "I swear, she's like the little devil sitting on my shoulder, except my angel always seems to be on a smoke break. She got me to agree to the most ridiculous bet…"

"Oh yeah? What's the bet?" Cash asks, a loose brown curl tumbling across his forehead.

I clap both hands over my mouth, eyes going wide. "Oh nooo," I laugh, "No, no, no. I'm not telling."

"Come on," he presses, tugging me just a little closer, "Tell me what the bet is, Porter."

"No, no. I can't," I insist, busying myself with another gulp of beer, "You'll think it's absolutely pathetic."

"Well, now you *have* to tell me," he grins. "I'll be the judge whether or not it's pathetic."

I throw up my hands, just tipsy enough to no longer give a shit. It's not like I'm ever going to see this guy again after tonight, right?

"Fine," I say, looking him square in the eye, "Allie bet me that I couldn't bring myself to have one random hookup before my vacation is over."

Cash stares at me. "That's it?" he asks.

"Well, yeah," I tell him.

A roar of laughter rises out of him, "How is that something you even have to bet on?" he crows, "I say it doesn't count as a vacation until you have at least one random hookup!"

"Well ex*cuse* me," I shoot back, "Looks like one of us is a lot more prone to one night stands than the other."

"What's wrong with one night stands?" Cash asks, setting his empty beer bottle down on the bar.

"Nothing… in theory," I mutter, suddenly bashful. I barely know this guy, but I already feel like there's nothing I can hide from him.

"Wait, wait," Cash says, spinning my bar stool around to face his. "You *have* had a one night stand before, haven't you?" His face is mere inches from mine now, our legs interlocked between us. Between my buzz and his proximity to me, I can barely put one word in front of another. But in the end, I don't have to. He can read the answer on my face, plain as day.

"You haven't…" he goes on, an expression of amazement so overwhelming, that it looks painful coming across his face.

"Got me," I smile timidly. He leans back in his seat, just looking at me. Self-consciousness washes over me, forcing me to avert my gaze. "That doesn't make me a zoo animal, so you can quit staring," I mutter.

"Sorry. My bad," he says, "I just can't quite believe it."

"No?" I reply, all stocked up on liquid courage. "Why's that?"

"Because you must have your pick of the litter, where guys are concerned," he says simply, "I mean…look at you."

"Well, you would know what that's like, huh?" I reply, so pleased by the compliment that I don't even mind blowing my spot.

"What, you like what you see?" he grins, pretending to strike a pose for me.

"Obviously," I laugh, resting my hand on his knee without thinking…but definitely not rushing to move it anytime soon.

"So we agree about one thing," he murmurs contemplatively, letting his hand fall on top of mine, "We each think the other is sexy as hell."

"Is that what I said?!" I laugh, blushing.

"I may have embellished a little," he replies, "But even though we're both attracted to each other, one of us is a lot more prone to one night stands than the other, right? What to do…"

I feel my pulse quicken as he rubs his thumb against my hand. Joking around about random hookups is one thing…but the fact remains that I've never done anything like that before. I don't have anything against sleeping with someone outside of a relationship, but I also don't know anything about this guy. Other than the fact that the mere pressure of his hand against mine is making me clench my thighs together, as pulses of desire ripple up through my body.

"Wouldn't that be something, if I knocked out my bet on the first night…" I say, trying to sound breezy. But the raging lust twisting my core rings out loud and clear through my voice.

"Is that what you want?" Cash asks, leaning into me as his hand moves slowly higher on my thigh.

"I…Well…" I stammer, savoring the feel of his fingers brushing against my thigh through the denim.

"You're blushing," he tells me, eyes gleaming with serious want. Up and up his hand strays, moving closer to that throbbing place between my legs. I have to swallow hard to keep from moaning, his hands feel so good on me.

"No kidding, I'm blushing," I breathe, "How are you not?"

"I'm just better at hiding it than you," he smiles. But he sets all joking aside the very next moment, stilling his hand just before it brushes against my sex. "Listen Maddie," he goes on, "I know we've been kidding around all night, but if you're not into this, or you've had too much to drink, or—"

"I haven't," I say hurriedly, "I mean, I am…into it."

"I need you to be one hundred percent sure," he says firmly, lifting his hands away from my body, "Especially if you've never had a one-off before. Hell, I'm not even sure if you could handle me, even just for a night."

I laugh, though my body is crying out for his touch. "I'm pretty sure I'd be able to handle you just fine, Hawthorne."

"Maybe," he shrugs, turning slightly away from me. "But I'm telling you right now, pretty sure isn't gonna cut it for me."

He's giving me an out. I can get up and walk away right now if I want to, no strings, no hard feelings. And every other day of my life leading up to this, with every other guy I've ever met, that's exactly what I'd do. But today, Cash is sitting in front of me. His scruffy, cut jaw pulsing as he bites back his want of me. His hazel eyes burning with both need and the restraint of it. His strong, expert hands resting resolutely on his knees, when they should be exploring every inch of me.

"Fuck it," I mutter fiercely, taking his sculpted face in my hands and closing the space between us.

In the second that it takes for me to bring my mouth to his, he's raced up to meet me in the moment. He catches my lips in his, as I open my mouth to him. The full firmness of his lips nearly takes my breath away. I wrap my arms behind his neck, steadying myself against him, as his tongue glides against mine. The taste of him dances across my tongue, and I'm drunker off him in a second, than I've managed to get all night. I take his bottom lip between my teeth, biting gently down. A low, soft groan rumbles at the very core of him, so deep that I can feel it where we connect at the mouth.

"How's that for one hundred percent sure?" I breathe, pulling back to train my blue eyes on him.

"Yeah. That'll do," he growls, his arms circling my slender waist.

It's only then, that I notice the catcalls rising up from the back of the bar. The group of bikers clustered around the pool table started cheering us on as we locked lips, and they have all kinds of dirty suggestions as to what we should do now.

"We seem to have an audience," I murmur.

"I'm not sure I should drive back to my place, after this many rounds…" Cash says, gritting his teeth. "But dammit, I'll carry you back if I have to."

I let my hands trail down his body, unthinking. They run over the firm panes of his chest, the perfect line of abs, and onward. Suddenly, I feel my fingertips brush against a staggering new development. I glance down, eyes widening as I take in the bulging length, threatening to tear straight through his jeans. That does it.

"I'm staying at the motel next door," I breathe, eyes locked on his.

"Why the hell didn't you say so?" he breathes, his voice husky with lust.

I stand up from my barstool, barely able to remain upright from the throbbing between my legs. As casually as possible, I lace my fingers through Cash's and pull him to standing. He plays along with my nonchalance, draping an arm across my shoulders as we turn to go. As the bikers start roaring their approval, we glance in unison over our shoulders and each give them the finger with our free hands. Our synchronized bird-flipping makes us whip around to face each other, smiling like a couple of lunatics. If our bodies are already this synced up, that bodes pretty well for the rest of the evening.

The second the bar door swings shut behind us, Cash's powerful hands grab hold of my hips. He swings me around and presses me up against the brick wall of the bar, kissing me hard as he holds me pinned there. I gasp as he shifts his hips, letting me feel his rigid cock right against my aching slit. Our tongues tangle as I bury my fingers in his thick, dark curls. The brick is rough against my bare shoulders, but I couldn't give less of a damn.

"Goddammit…" Cash rasps, brushing a lock of hair away from my face as he looks down at me in the red neon light. "I've wanted to do that from the second I laid eyes on you."

"Really?" I breathe, "Could've fooled me."

"Like I said, I know how to hide things better than you," he smiles, running his hands down my sides as he brings his lips to my neck.

I let my head fall back against the brick as he kisses deeply along my throat, dizzy with needing to feel more of him.

"Come on, Hawthorne," I urge with a grin, breaking away across the gravel, "Before the crazy motel biddy sees us."

"I'm not even gonna ask what the hell you're talking about," Cash says, taking off after me across the lot.

I dash out ahead of him, feeling for the world like I'm sixteen years old again. How can something so illicit feel so light, so easy? Cash catches up to me in no time, ducking down and scooping me into a fireman's carry.

"Cash!" I cry out, "What—?"

"Army training. What can I tell you?" he laughs, racing toward the motel. "This pretty damn near feels like a life or death situation, after all…"

He skids to a stop just outside my door and sets me upright as I fumble for my keycard. I can barely get the thing in, my hands are trembling so hard. But the second that lock clicks open, we tumble through the doorway and slam it shut on the rest of the world. Our hands find each other's bodies in the near pitch-blackness, lifting off layers of clothing as we stagger across the unfamiliar room.

I feel my feet go out from under me as I trip over my huge suitcase. The bed rises up to meet me as I fall, bringing Cash down on top of me. We laugh through kissing at the slapstick moment, but soon the only sound I can make is a low, shuddering moan. I fall back against the mattress, wearing nothing but my panties as Cash kneels over me. That same neon glow flashes against his bare skin, illuminating every perfectly cut muscle. Every line of ink. And as he tugs down his black briefs, I finally catch a glimpse of his staggering, irresistible cock.

"You know something?" I gasp, reaching to run my hands along that hard, pulsating length. "I think I could get used to this one night stand thing…"

But my words cut out as he slips my panties down over the rise of my ass and lowers himself to me.

"Maddie," he rasps, "I'm gonna make you wish for a whole lot more than one night…"

I let my knees fall apart, opening myself to him. I can feel the swollen tip of him pressed flush against my wetness. I'm holding onto his broad, muscled shoulders for dear life, craving the feel of him deep inside me. But instead of driving his cock into my very core, he starts kissing along my neck, between my breasts, over the valley of my taut stomach, further and further down, until—

"Oh, Jesus Christ," I gasp, raking my fingers along his back as I feel his warm breath against my slick sex.

"Told you," he growls in the dizzying darkness—his last words before I feel his expert tongue running along the length of me.

If this is what random hookups are like, I think in my blissful delight, *I'll stick to them for the rest of my life.*

Chapter Three

The next morning...

"Shit, shit..." I mutter, as my phone begins chirping incessantly from the other room.

Still clutching the tangled motel sheet to my naked body, I dart out of the bathroom and snatch up the noisy device. I'd totally forgotten that I set an early alarm. Blinking blearily at the bright screen, I hurry to silence the thing before it wakes up my unexpected roommate.

I hold my breath as Cash rolls onto his back on the narrow bed, but his own breathing remains slow and shallow. He's still fast asleep. My gaze is arrested as I catch sight of him in the early morning light. Try as I might, I can't look away from the rise and fall of his sculpted, ink-covered chest. Two rows of perfectly formed abs roll like hills along his torso, giving way to the muscular "V" of his waist. And just below that...

"Oh my god," I squeak in a whisper, my eyes going wide at the sight of his prodigious morning wood, holding up the motel comforter like a tent pole. "Oh my god, oh my god..."

I dash back into the bathroom and close the door behind me, chest rising and falling like mad. The full weight of what happened between me and Cash last night is finally hitting me. This is far from the first time I've slept with someone, but it is the first time for *multiple* other things. Or rather, multiples of one very wonderful thing. Why didn't anyone tell me sex could be like that? I would have been having much more of it this whole time! With, admittedly, far more skillful partners.

My cell buzzes in my hand, and I glance down to see that I have a new text from Allie.

Allie: Miss you already! Good luck on your mission xx

I swallow a laugh and text back.

Me: Too late ;)

Allie pounces on the bait at once...

Allie: What do you mean, too late???

With my heart lodged in my throat, I peek around the bathroom door. Cash Hawthorne is still fast asleep in my bed. Allie will never believe that I've actually spent the night with him…unless I offer her some proof. I raise my phone and snap a pic of his slumbering form. Not exactly good morning-after etiquette, I know, but I can always plead ignorance of the one night stand rules of engagement if pressed. I send the pic to Allie in a message, and receive an immediate, and exuberant, reply.

Allie:
!!!!!!!!!!!!!!!!!!!!!!!!!!!!!!!!!!!!!!!
!!!!!!!!!!!!!!!!

Me: Yep. Mission accomplished :)

Allie: I've never been so proud of you. Ever.

Me: Thanks? I think?

Allie: Who is he?!

Me: Oh, just some handsome stranger I picked up at the bar last night...

Allie: STFU WHO ARE YOU EVEN

Me: I don't know what to tell you, lady.

Allie: Oh, only EVERY SINGLE DETAIL.

Me: I will, just as soon as I figure out what to do about the babe in my bed.

Allie: I have a few suggestions...

Me: Oh, I'm sure. Talk to you soon, you terrible influence.

Allie: Love you! Have good sex!

I shake my head at the phone and creep back into the motel room proper. As quietly as I can, I weed my clothes out from Cash's and slip back into them. My plan was to get on the road first thing in the morning today. I wasn't expecting to factor a little morning-after discussion into the schedule.

My stomach flips as I try and figure out what I should even say to Cash before I go. *"Thanks for the awesome fuck, see you never"? "Gotta go, have a nice life with your incredible cock"?* Nothing I can think of quite does the trick. Maybe I should just duck out before he wakes up and spare us both the moment of awkwardness? I'm sure I'll just say the wrong thing and ruin what was an incredible night. What I really want is to see him again, but I can't tell him that. I'll just seem needy and clingy—anathema to a lone wolf type like him, I'm sure. One thing is certain—I need to decide on a course of action before my gorgeous bedmate wakes up.

Before I can overthink this any further, I grab the complementary notepad and pen from the bedside table and scrawl the first thing that comes to mind:

Cash—It was wonderful to meet you. Take care. MP

And with that, I grab my suitcase and head for the door. I grant myself one last look at Cash Hawthorne's gorgeous sleeping face before going. I don't know much about one night stands, but I know there's no way I should be feeling this attached to mine. Maybe I should stay after all? Grab some coffee with him, trade numbers?

No, I think resolutely, forcing myself out the door, *Leave it be, Maddie. Don't try to make this into something it's not. It'll just hurt when he doesn't feel the same way.*

I slide my keycard into the drop box outside the office, hurrying away before the blue-haired sentry reappears. The last thing I want to do is explain to her why housekeeping is going to find a man among my bedsheets later today.

My sex-scrambled brain gets turned around more than once on the second leg of my road trip, adding four whole hours onto my drive. By the time I get my bearings and turn onto the long, dusty road leading off to the address my mother provided me, it's late in the day. My stomach cramps with hunger and my hangover pounds away at my skull. At least my physical discomfort distracts me from the curious pangs that keep tugging at my heartstrings. It must just be because I'm unused to sex outside of a relationship, but I already feel myself starting to miss Cash…which is *insane*, I know. Not to mention lame as hell. But what's a girl to do?

I steer my ancient Honda down the winding road as tall, leafy trees arch overhead. I've never seen this alleged lake house before, or even visited my mom's old hometown. I have no idea what to expect…but it's definitely not what's actually waiting around the bend, that's for damn sure.

My jaw falls open as a huge, gorgeously built home appears in my field of vision. A wide, shaded veranda encircles the three-story wooden home, and the turquoise blue water of a pristine lake filters through the tree line behind it. A sprawling lawn has been cleared around the house, dotted with vegetable and flower gardens, bocce and badminton courts, and a hot tub and outdoor shower. Green shutters and dark stained wood lend an air of gravity and class to the rustic paradise—all told, this place is absolutely incredible.

The only question is…what the hell is my mom doing, renting out a palace like this? She doesn't exactly rake in the dough as an artist. Something's off, here.

I spot a few cars lining the driveway and park mine behind them, filling my lungs with crisp lake air as I step outside. Blinking into the bright, dappled sunlight, I make my way toward the front door of the impressive house, climbing the flight of wooden steps that lead up to the porch. I'm just about to close my fingers around the doorknob, when a flutter of motion catches the corner of my eye.

"Jesus Christ!" I yelp, falling back against the door. A lithe, contorted body is pretzeled there on the porch, halfway hidden by the shadow of the house. And upon second glance, I see that it's a very familiar pretzel, indeed. "Sophie, you scared the shit out of me," I gasp.

"Oh. Hey, Maddie," replies my middle sister, glancing up at me from her elaborate posture. "One sec, I'm just finishing up my practice."

"What are you practicing, exactly?" I ask her, cocking my head, "How to fit a corpse into a suitcase?"

She untangles her limbs with a sigh, and comes to sitting on a muted red mat. Her wavy caramel blonde hair is pulled into a bun, her long limbs glistening with the exertion of her exercise. I'm suddenly feeling very self-conscious of my smeared makeup and slouchy clothes—but that's always sort of the effect that the effortlessly gorgeous Sophie has on me.

"It's yoga, Maddie," she says now, already bored with me, "Surely you've heard of it."

And just like that, my little sister and I are off to a shaky start. As per usual. Sophia has always been the most serious Porter sister, and my constant efforts to lighten the mood only ever seem to make things worse. And what with my pounding hangover and baffled heart, I can't really muster up the energy to keep our interaction sunny.

"Did you know this place was going to be a mansion?" I ask her, crossing my arms, "There's no way Mom can be affording this easily."

"Since when has Mom ever bothered to run anything past us?" Sophie shrugs, rolling up her mat. "I'm sure it's fine."

My mouth turns down at the corners. Why am I always the only one worrying about the big picture around here? I'm about to keep pressing for details when a flutter of ash blonde hair—nearly white in its lightness—appears between the trees at the edge of the yard, catching my eye. Speaking of pictures...

"Is that Anna?" I ask Sophie, squinting across the grassy expanse.

"Who else?" she replies, following my gaze in the direction of our youngest sister. "She's been wandering around the woods with her camera for hours. I don't think she's said three words all morning."

"Sounds about right," I say, watching as Annabel's willowy form crouches down to snap a shot of some Queen Anne's Lace. Of all us Porter women, Anna's the quietest. In fact, I'd say she's the *only* quiet one among us. It isn't that she's shy, necessarily—just a girl of few words.

"Hey, Annie Leibowitz!" Sophie calls, shattering the serene afternoon silence, "Look who's finally here!"

Anna looks up with her enormous blue eyes, looking for the world like a startled deer. Sometimes I think she forgets the rest of the world exists when she's peering through her camera lens. She turns and lopes toward us across the yard, a placid smile on her face.

"Hi Maddie," she says, climbing the porch steps two at a time. Her pale legs go on for miles. When did she go from being my scrappy, scabby-kneed little sister to a grown woman? "Did you get lost or something? The day's half gone."

"Probably just dragged her feet all the way here," Sophie mutters, "Not that I blame you."

"Uh-huh," I reply, refusing to engage in her bantering. I'm here because Mom asked me to come, and because my bosses forced me to finally take my saved-up vacation days, not to bicker with my little sisters for two weeks.

"Some place, right?" Anna says, beaming around the property, "I can't believe we get to stay here."

"The question is *how* do, we get to stay here," I reply, planting my hands on my hips. "I know we've never necessarily been hurting for money, but this seems a little exorbitant for four people. Don't you think?"

Sophie's eyes sparkle mischievously. "Oh, it's not just four of us," she tells me.

"What do you mean?" I shoot back.

"You don't know?" Anna asks.

"Of course she doesn't. Mom didn't say anything about it to us," Sophie replies.

"Guys. What is it I don't know?" I ask, exasperated.

"Ask Mom," Sophie replies, "I'm sure she'll explain everything."

"Sophie, what—" I press, but don't get any further. Right on cue, the front door swings open, and I find myself wrapped up in the airy but ardent embrace of my mother, Robin Porter.

"Finally! All my girls are here," she gushes in her light, bell-like voice. Thick golden blonde curls fly every which way as she greets me, the gold-flecked blue eyes she passed along to her daughters shining with happy tears.

"Mom, Hey," I reply, returning her hug, "Sophie and Anna were just telling me—"

"Just look at you," she cuts me off, holding me at arm's length for inspection. "I love the short hair! So becoming, Maddie. Have you lost a little baby fat since the last time I saw you? Oh, you must have. And there's something else different, too. A sort of *glow*. I can't put my finger on it…"

I step away from her, hoping that the "something else" isn't the lingering sexed-up flush of last night's escapades. Just in case, I change the subject as quickly as I can.

"Mom, Sophie just told me it isn't just us staying here." I cut to the chase, "What is she talking about?"

"Come inside, let me show you around," my mom trills, seeming not to have heard me. I swallow down my annoyance with her habit of not listening when other people speak. After 24 years, I'm pretty accustomed to her talking right over everyone else. Like little ducklings, my sisters and I fall in behind our mother as she glides into the impressive house.

A huge great room opens up before us, its far wall an enormous window that looks out onto the deck and lake beyond. I'm struck dumb by the gorgeousness of the view, and the fine craftsmanship that's gone into every detail of the home's decor. Midcentury modern furniture and fixtures populate the high-ceilinged space, which includes a fully stocked kitchen, breakfast nook, and fireplace. The combination of rustic and sleek touches is truly striking. There must be at least half a dozen bedrooms upstairs, judging by the size of this place. But then, who's occupying them besides us?

"Don't you just love it?" Mom asks rapturously, doing a little spin around the great room. Her long bohemian skirts fans out around her, the bangles around her wrists jangling. "Every single detail was handpicked. John really does have incredible taste. And not just in design, either. You should see the wine cellar—"

"John?" I cut her off sharply, "Who's John?"

"Oh!" she exclaims, her hand flying to her chest, "You haven't met John yet! He was here just a second ago…"

"OK, but who is he?" I ask again, trailing my mom as she peers around the ground floor.

"He owns the house," Mom replies distractedly. "He built it, actually. Incredible, right?"

"Yeah. Sure. So, what is this—like a house share or something?" I ask, exasperated, "Is he running a B&B, or—?"

"Here he is!" Mom cries out, clapping her hands together as the door to the porch swings open into the kitchen.

The man who steps inside has to stoop to keep from smacking his head on the door frame. He's absolutely huge—at least 6' 5", and built like an ox. His arms and legs are bulky with muscle, his stance combative. His face is halfway hidden beneath a thick brown beard, flecked with white. His defined brow is deeply creased, and his resting expression is a standoffish scowl. But the second he sees the four Porter woman standing around the kitchen, his eyes crinkle into a benevolent, if reserved, smile.

"The whole brood is finally here," says the enormous man, shucking off his green baseball cap now that he's inside.

"Yep!" my Mom chirps happily, "Maddie, this is John. John, Maddie."

"Nice to meet you, Maddie," he says, extending his free hand to me.

"And you," I offer, as John's plowshare of a hand swallows mine whole. "It's a pleasure I wasn't expecting. I actually didn't realize there would be anyone but us Porter ladies here."

John lets my hand drop, glancing back at my mother. "Didn't you tell them?" he asks.

"I could have sworn I mentioned it…" Mom drawls, her freckled forehead furrowing slightly. "At least, I meant to."

"It's totally cool," I go on, "I just didn't realize, is all. Mom's never been a huge stickler for details."

"That's our Robin for you," John says with a short laugh, looking warmly at my mom. She gives him a little bump with her hip, clucking her tongue at him. I glance at my sisters with raised eyebrows, but they don't look as surprised as I feel. Why do I get the sense that I'm still lacking some information here?

"So. How did this house sharing arrangement come about?" I ask, as my mom goes to the fridge and produces a pitcher of lemonade.

"Well," John says, sitting down at the long kitchen table and kicking off his boots, "Your mom and I go way back. We both grew up here, you know. Went all the way through high school together before she pissed off to the big city."

"I hardly call going to art school 'pissing off', but that's the gist of it," Mom laughs airily, setting the pitcher down before John, who helps himself to a glass. "When I decided to come back here and get in touch with my roots, John was one of the first people I reached out to. He's one of my oldest, best friends."

"That's one way to put it," John cuts in, wiping his mouth with the back of his hand. "To tell you the truth, your mom here was my One Who Got Away."

"Huh," I say flatly, as Sophie tries not to laugh at my surprise, "That's…interesting. And now you're, uh, renting out part of this house to her? To us?"

"Renting?" John says, looking almost offended, "I'd never take money from a friend. Especially not this one. Your mother's been staying here at the house as my guest. And now you girls are, too."

There it is. The little piece of information that changes the entire nature of this getaway—the less-than-pleasant surprise I knew would be waiting in store for me, courtesy of my mother. She hasn't just been visiting her hometown these past few months—she's been living here with an enigmatic mountain man, who seems to have quite the thing for her. And from the way she's beaming at him across the kitchen table, I can only assume the feeling is mutual.

"There's one last free bedroom waiting for you upstairs," Mom tells me, completely oblivious to my displeasure with her. "Between your sisters and John's boys, we're at full capacity now!"

"Oh...You have kids, too?" I ask John, trying to keep up with all the new developments going off like firecrackers around me. On top of everything else, there are going to be a bunch of rug rats underfoot?

"Yeah," John says, heaving a deep sigh as he settles back in his chair, "They're all around here somewhere. Could never keep track of 'em, to be perfectly honest."

"Right," I smile weakly, trying to keep calm, "I, uh...I'm just gonna step out back and get some air, OK? See the rest of the property."

"Take your time!" my mom says cheerfully, "You're on vacation, after all. Relax. I'll get started on dinner in a bit."

"Thanks for the heads up," I hiss at Sophie as I pass her on the way to the back door.

"You got as much warning as any of us," she replies, following me outside. Anna's already disappeared somewhere, as she always does.

I shut the patio door tightly behind me and shove a hand through my dark blonde hair.

"What the hell is going on?" I whisper, glancing back at Mom and John mooning over each other at the kitchen table.

"Mom's having a little love affair, I guess," Sophie shrugs, "I didn't particularly like finding out this way, but—"

"With him?!" I cut her off, "I mean, look at him! He's like, a lumberjack or something. He's not her type at all."

"He's a contractor, not a lumberjack," Sophie corrects me, "And we don't know what her type is, if she has one. We only ever saw her with Dad."

"Exactly," I reply fiercely, feeling suddenly close to tears, "She loved Dad more than anything. Smart, funny, put-together Dad. This guy is nothing like him."

"Maybe that's part of the appeal," Sophie says, walking ahead of me down the patio steps that lead toward the lake. "Mom obviously came back here to take her mind off losing Dad. It makes sense that she's drawn to someone totally unlike him."

"How can you be so calm about this?!" I exclaim, catching her slender wrist in my hand and turning her around to face me. "Dad just died, Sophie. This is—"

"Dad died three years ago," she says firmly, doling out the tough love I always need and never want from her. "We need to support Mom in trying to move on.

We need to try and move on ourselves too, Maddie. Especially you."

"It's not like I haven't been trying," I say softly, my voice cracking with emotion. I feel the fight go out of me as anger gives way to upset. Fat, salty tears start to roll down my cheeks, and I feel Sophie's arms enclose me.

"Hey now," she says, her voice warm and soothing, "I know you've been trying. I know. Just breathe, Maddie."

"God, I miss him," I whisper, letting my head rest on my little sister's shoulder.

"We all do," she says, brushing the hair away from my face. "And we probably always will. But we've still got to try our best to be happy, right?"

"When did you get all rational and wise and shit?" I ask her, laughing through tears.

"Drama school is basically one carefully controlled nervous breakdown," she says, matter-of-factly, "I've worked through a lot of shit. You should try taking a clown class—it does wonders for your world view."

"I have no idea whether you're joking or not," I say, shaking my head.

"Me either," she smiles, brushing a tear off my cheek. "Now pull yourself together. I think we have company."

My ears perk up as the sound of a revving engine floats across the lawn. Sophie and I look over toward a wide path leading off into the woods—the sound seems to be coming from over there. As we watch, a cloud of dust starts advancing on us from afar, at the center of which is a black ATV.

"Bet that's one of John's boys," Sophie says, narrowing her eyes.

"That's hardly a boy," I point out. I'd been assuming that his sons would be kids for some reason, but the person atop that growling machine is a grown man. And that hardly puts me at ease. "Have you met them yet?"

"No," she says, rolling her eyes, "I guess they don't care much for the company of women. They've been making themselves scarce since I got here yesterday. This one showed up just before you, hopped on an ATV, and took off into the woods."

"Charming," I mutter, crossing my arms as the ATV roars our way.

"He doesn't seem to be slowing down…" I hear Anna say from over my shoulder. I jump at her sudden appearance behind me.

"We need to get you a cowbell or something," I tell her, watching as the loud machine comes charging out of the woods, headed our way.

"Is he going to stop?" Sophie asks, backing away as the ATV bears down.

"I have no idea," I reply, grabbing Anna's hand and yanking her out of its path. She may be a legal adult, but I'll never stop thinking of her as a kid I need to protect.

The three of us let out high-pitched shrieks as the vehicle turns sharply in our direction. It skids out in a clear arc, tearing up the cultivated grass in its wake, sending pebbles and dirt flying at us as we cover our faces. I glare up heatedly as the engine cuts out, displaced bits of lawn settling all around us.

"What the hell was that!" I cry out as the towering figure swings himself down from the ATV. "Last I checked, running over your houseguests isn't exactly good manners."

John's son turns his helmeted face in my direction, though I can't see his eyes through the visor. He's nearly as tall as his dad, and wears a simple black tee shirt with dark jeans. For a long moment, he stands perfectly still, just staring at me. What is this, some kind of intimidation technique? Trying to show me who's boss around here? I lift my chin defiantly, unwilling to give any ground. He raises his arms to lift off the helmet…and it's only then that I notice his full sleeve of tattoos. Before I can process another thought, he removes the helmet and shakes out his dark curly hair, backlit by the crystal blue lake. His unmistakable hazel eyes bore mercilessly into mine.

"*You* wanna talk about manners?" Cash growls at me, his gorgeous features hard and unreadable.

"Oh shit," I whisper, feeling the breath rush out of my lungs. Just when I thought this vacation couldn't get any more twisted…

Chapter Four

I gape up into Cash Hawthorne's stony face, attempting to wrap my mind around what the fuck, exactly, is happening here.

"What…How are you…What?" I stammer, as the figment from last night's salacious dream takes a swinging step my way.

"Didn't mean to spook you," he says, lips twisting into an unconvincing smile. "You city girls are awfully jumpy."

"And you country boys are hard to track down," Sophie says from over my shoulder, "Which of John's boys are you?"

"I'm Cash," he replies, his hard eyes still trained on me.

"I'm Sophia," she tells him flatly, "The doe-eyed one is Annabel. And the short one right there is—"

"Madeleine," I say softly, holding out my hand for Cash to shake. I'm embarrassed to see that it's trembling, "Madeleine Porter".

Cash glances down at my hand, then back up at my face, his wry smile unflinching. Even I'm baffled by my outstretched hand—pretending not to know him was my first instinct. But did I just do something egregiously wrong?

"Right," Cash says, ignoring my hand completely.

"Let's… go see if Mom needs any help in the kitchen," Anna suggests, looping her arm through Sophie's.

"God yes," Sophie mutters, turning to go, "Hell, we could use a knife to cut through all this male ego clogging up the air."

My little sisters hurry back into the house, leaving me squared off against Cash, the man I spent last night fucking every which way. The man who also happens to be the son of my mom's one-time—and likely present-day—fling. The man who is currently looking at me in such a way that tells me I seriously missed the mark with my morning-after etiquette.

"I think I need to sit down…" I say quietly, feeling my knees turn to water.

"Suit yourself," Cash shrugs, shaking out his sweat-slicked curls. "You're our house guest. Apparently."

"This is your house…" I echo, trying to make any of this sink in. "But then what…what were you doing at that bar last night? If you live here, I mean?"

"I don't live here," Cash says impatiently.

"But you just said—"

"My dad asked my brothers and I to come out here for a couple of weeks. Bit of male bonding or some shit," he cuts me off, "I was on my way here when I stopped for a drink. Same as you, I imagine."

"So…Did know anything about this?" I ask him, sinking down onto the porch steps. "About us being here? About me—?"

"What do you think?" Cash shoots back.

"I don't *know* what I think, that's why I'm asking you," I reply tersely, "Could you drop the asshole act and talk to me?"

"What act?" he laughs shortly, setting his helmet down on the seat of the ATV, "This is just me, babe. Don't know what to tell you."

"You can tell me why you're acting like a jerk all of a sudden," I say, wrapping my arms around my knees. "I'm sorry if I didn't handle this morning well. You know I don't have much experience with the whole—
"

"I honestly couldn't care less," he says evenly. I don't know him nearly well enough to tell if he's lying to me. "But hey, let's maybe not mention the fact that we fucked like animals all last night around our families, yeah? Might make them a little uncomfortable."

I stare up at him, mind reeling along with my heart. "So, what… You're saying we just forget it ever happened? Pretend we've never met?"

"Isn't that what you want?" he asks, eyes hard on my face, "I mean, wasn't that the plan when you left this morning?"

I bite my lip, willing myself not to start crying again. The only reason I left without saying goodbye, was that I didn't want to get my hopes up of something more with Cash. I didn't want to ruin what happened between us by making an ass of myself the next morning. But would you look at that? I seem to have done it anyway.

"I'm really sorry, Cash," I say imploringly, "Please, let me explain. I don't want you to hate me—"

"Maddie, for the love of Christ, don't turn this into a fucking soap opera. I don't hate you," he snaps, exasperated, "I told you. I don't care. Just drop it, OK?"

I hold my tongue, trying to see past the steely mask of indifference he's wearing. We may not know each other very well, but this isn't the man I spent all of last night with. He's icing me out. He thinks I bailed this morning because I wasn't into it, and he doesn't want to look bad. What we have here, as the movies say, is a big ol' failure to communicate. But something tells me that communication isn't going to be Cash Hawthorne's strong suit.

"Goddammit, Cash!" John roars from the kitchen doorway. I spin around to see him towering above us on the patio, fists clenched.

"Hey Pop," Cash nods, producing a pack of cigarettes from his back pocket.

"Don't 'hey Pop' me," John growls, "What the hell did you do to my fucking lawn?"

Cash glances back at the semicircular skid marks the ATV cut through the grass. "Oh yeah. You're right," he says, lighting up a smoke. I try not to fixate on his lips as they cradle his fresh cigarette.

"Fix it," John snaps, "And put that fucking thing out. That habit will kill you one day."

"What?" Cash replies, feigning amazement, "Smoking is *bad* for you?!"

"Maddie," John says to me, forcing a deep breath into his lungs, "I can't slug him without having to foot the bill for a decade of therapy. You do it for me, OK?"

"Little late for that," Cash mutters under his breath, taking a long drag on his cigarette.

For a second, John fixes a look of pure rage on his oldest son. My body goes stiff with apprehension, and I halfway expect John to launch himself off the patio and right at Cash's form. But thankfully, the eldest Hawthorne manages to take a breath, turns on his heel, and marches away. Before I can say another word, Cash hops back on the ATV and races in the other direction, toward the garage—cigarette still held between his lips. I, for my part, stand rooted to the ground, looking plaintively after him as he goes.

"Well," I mutter, eyeing the deep tire ruts left in the fresh-cut grass, "It wouldn't be a Porter family vacation if it wasn't totally fucked."

I spend the rest of the evening intently chopping up vegetables and herbs for dinner, trying my damnedest to get a hold of my runaway mind. Of all the men in the world, I had to have my first one night stand—and best sex of my life, I may add—with the son of my mom's new "man friend"? What are the chances, even—a bajillion to one? Now, I get to spend the next two weeks under Cash's withering gaze, pretending it doesn't hurt like hell that he's acting like we're strangers. I know we only got to spend one night together, but he doesn't feel like a stranger to me. I felt more connected to and engaged with him than I have with anyone in years. That can't just mean nothing, can it?

Maybe if I'd just told him all that, instead of leaving him a note like an asshole, we wouldn't be in this predicament. Of course, there's the whole weirdness of our parents maybe being an item, but I honestly don't buy that my mom can stay interested in this new guy for more than a couple weeks. Tops. By the time we're ready to hit the road, she'll have moved onto her next flight of fancy. That's always been her way.

"Maddie," my mom trills, lifting a huge tray of baked potatoes from the oven, "Why don't you go round up the boys? Everything'll be ready in a sec."

I let the kitchen knife go clattering to the floor, looking up at her with startled eyes.

"Oh. I don't. I mean—" I stammer, "I don't really know where they are…"

"I think they're down by the lake," Anna replies, dropping a dozen golden dinner rolls into a basket.

"What, do you need a chaperone to face the big bad boys?" Sophie teases me, sipping a glass of Merlot at the table, "Come on. I'll go with you."

I give in and trail Sophie out the door. I may as well accept the fact that this week is going to be awkward as hell. No use fighting it.

"I still haven't met the younger guys," Sophie says over her shoulder, traipsing down toward the dock in her bare feet. "They've been making themselves pretty damn scarce. Not that I have high hopes, having met Cash."

"Yeah," I laugh nervously, crossing my arms, "He seems like kind of a dick, right?"

"Total dick. Pretty hot though," she replies casually.

"S-sorry?" I sputter.

"What? He *is*," she replies, "Did you see those tattoos? And that hair? God lord. It's like if Jon Snow and Thor had a super sexy, tatted-up love child. Not sure how that would work biologically, but—"

"I mean, yeah, he's pretty attractive…" I allow, "But I mean, he's kind of off-limits, right? All the boys are. What with Mom and John's history and everything?"

"Whoa, *whoa*. I wasn't planning on jumping him or anything, Maddie," Sophie laughs, "Unless you think he'd be into it, that is."

I bite my tongue, feeling my heart clench painfully in my chest. There's no denying that Sophie is the real beauty of the family. With her long, wavy hair, big blue eyes, and slender, graceful frame, she's every bit the conventional knockout. When we were in high school together, I had fellow senior guys asking me to set them up with Sophie, then a freshman. She's never given her beauty a second thought, or made me feel inferior on purpose, but she's also never failed to get any guy she wanted. So if she turns her sights on Cash…

"Christ, Maddie. I'm kidding," Sophie goes on, as we draw up before the dock.

"Oh. Right," I reply flatly. "I knew that."

"We need to get you drunk ASAP tonight," Sophie laughs, "The rat race is turning you into something of a downer, my dear."

I put on my best attempt at a casual expression and follow Sophie toward the end of the platform, where a broad shouldered young man I have yet to meet stands looking out across the lake. This must be another of the guys we're supposed to be rounding up, though the other two Hawthorne brothers are nowhere to be seen.

"Hey there," Sophie calls to him.

But he doesn't acknowledge the greeting.

"Maybe he didn't hear you?" I whisper, stopping short.

Sophie narrows her eyes at the built young man standing before us and marches on ahead. "Hey," she says, tapping the guy on his cut shoulder, "What's up?"

He shrugs off her hand and raises it in a gesture that clearly says, "Shut up." Sophie's face goes red with embarrassment and anger, but it soon becomes clear what he's focusing so intently on instead of her.

Straight ahead of us, two svelte bodies churn and chop the water as they race to the dock. Powerful, precise limbs propel them forward toward us. Their pace is matched, and the two are neck and neck as they approach. Sophie and I leap back as they barrel toward the dock, sending a soaking spray of lake water our way. As we look on, Cash and another of his brothers grab hold of the wooden platform and hoist themselves up out of the water, and I for one feel as if I'm being swept away.

Water courses in rivulets over Cash's impeccably muscled body, and I can't tear my gaze away. As he straightens up, I run my eyes along his cut torso, down to where his swim trunks rest dangerously low on his waist. My core twists with longing as he runs a hand through his soaking wet hair, each muscle rippling with the smallest of motions.

And I'm not the only one staring, either.

Sophie has gone stock still beside me, her eyes hard and fast not on Cash, but on the brother he emerged from the water beside. The color has gone completely out of her cheeks, and my normally ebullient sister is suddenly silent. What's that about?

"Well? Who had the best time, Finn?" Cash demands of the brother we first encountered on the dock.

"Couldn't tell, lost count. But it looked like a tie," Finn replies.

"No such thing," scoffs the brother Sophie's got her eyes trained on. "Do over."

"Maybe tomorrow, Luke. If you're a really good boy," Cash laughs, reaching for the pack of cigarettes waiting for him on the dock. Turning, he catches sight of Sophie and I...and doesn't even blink.

"What're you, afraid to lose to your little brother?" the other man returns, though he certainly doesn't look little to me. He's at least as tall as Cash, though more clean-cut—with only a couple of tattoos and close-cropped dark hair.

"Nah. We've just got *guests*," Cash replies, practically spitting the last word as he whips out and lights a cigarette.

The other two Hawthorne brothers look up, as if noticing us for the first time. The one called Luke barely gives me a second glance, but he catches Sophie's eye at once. A flicker of something like curiosity passes through his deep brown eyes, though it passes soon enough. The third brother, who looks to be the youngest, can't even be bothered to acknowledge our presence.

Looks like questionable first impressions run in the family.

"What can we do for you girls?" Cash asks, taking a long drag of his cigarette. He's doing a parody of being cordial, and it's getting on my last nerve.

"Dinner's ready," I inform him, "Mom sent us down to get you."

"We don't really do family dinners around here," Cash goes on, condescendingly.

"We're more of a pizza and beer family, ourselves," Luke puts in.

I wait for Sophie to make some kind of snappy comeback, as she always does…but the cat has yet to release her tongue. I draw myself up to my full height—which, granted, isn't much—and try to sound assertive.

"Well, we're not doing things your way tonight," I tell the trio of strapping young bucks standing before me, "We've gone out of our way to make a meal, and you three are going to join us. Sound good?"

"Christ," the youngest brother speaks at last, tossing his sweep of ash brown hair away from his eyes, "I didn't know we were gonna get the full June Cleaver treatment."

"Don't be an ass, Finn," Luke snaps. Apparently, he's the moral compass of this little tribe. "Come on. I'm not going to complain about a home cooked meal for once."

He strides past us toward the house, and Sophie goes well out of her way to avoid his gaze before following. Finn shrugs and follows suit—I get the feeling that he's more of a nihilist than an asshole. That just leaves me and Cash, alone again. I watch as he nurses his cigarette, in no hurry to move.

"You coming?" I ask him, watching his full lips close around the filter of his cig.

"In a minute," he says, looking out across the lake.

"Your brothers seem…Uh…Charming," I offer, not very convincingly, "I didn't know you were the oldest. I guess we have that in common, huh?"

"You didn't really stick around long enough to find out, did you?" Cash replies. Clearly, he's never going to let me live down my exit this morning. But instead of gushing about how sorry I am, I decide to give him a taste of his own medicine.

"Yeah," I drawl, dropping my voice an octave and giving an exaggerated shrug, "My policy has always been hit 'em and quit 'em. You get me, bro?"

"…What?" Cash replies flatly, raising an eyebrow.

"You know, man," I go on, "Can't be lettin' bitches get all attached and shit. I'm not a one-man kind of girl, you feel me?"

The corner of Cash's mouth lifts ever so slightly as my bro impression picks up steam. It's a tiny crack in his armor, a slight warming of his oh-so-cold shoulder treatment.

"Shit though," I go on, "I landed me one sweet piece of ass last night. If I wasn't a total idiot, I would have bought that boy breakfast in the morning… Maybe let him know that he was right about me wanting more than one night."

"Is that so?" Cash replies, his voice low and rasping.

"It is," I tell him, my act evaporating at once.

"Well," he goes on, that crooked smile widening ever-so-slightly. "That's good to know."

I hold my breath as he takes a step toward me, flicking his cigarette into the lake. He closes the space between us, catching my chin in his hand. We're hidden from sight by the gathering twilight, and I feel my knees start go weak with anticipation.

"You realize, though…" he growls, as I let my hands fall on his water-slicked chest, "That if anything else happens between us, you still won't have had a one night stand?"

"I think I can live with that," I whisper, tilting my face toward his.

His hands slide down my back, tugging me hard against his body. Every inch of me that's pressed to him is screaming with delight, both present and remembered.

"Well…We'll just have to see what happens, then," he murmurs, sliding his hands down over the rise of my ass. His lips brush against my neck, sending a shudder down my spine—

"Maddie! Cash!" I hear Sophie call from the deck, her voice high and strangled, "Come on already! It's time to eat."

I take a stumbling leap away from Cash as he looks on in amusement.

"Coming!" I cry out, scrambling up the dock.

"Already?" Cash teases, "I barely even touched you."

I let myself laugh at his crude joke, glad that there might be hope for our relationship yet—whatever the hell that relationship may be.

"You have to admit," he goes on, throwing a brotherly arm over my shoulders as we trudge toward the house, "This whole thing is pretty fucking hilarious."

"Oh yeah," I drawl, rolling my eyes, "It's a real laugh riot."

Chapter Five

As all eight Porters and Hawthornes settle down around the dinner table, I don't think anyone is oblivious to how bizarre our little gathering is. Anyone, that is, besides my mother—who serves out generous helpings to everyone with a contented smile on her face. Robin Porter is the epitome of adaptable. I swear, she could get comfy in a nudist colony, cultish commune, or post-apocalyptic hellscape if she had to. She's a woman who knows how to go with the flow, even if everyone around her is flailing in the current.

"So nice to have everyone here at last," she beams around the table. "Have all you kids gotten to know each other by now?"

"More or less," Cash grins, letting his knee brush against mine under the table. I swallow hard, trying to ignore the jolt of sensation that even this little contact sends through me. Cash and I have gotten to know each other, all right. At least in the biblical sense. What would the rest of this bizarro Brady Bunch think, if they knew the truth about us?

"Glad you kids are all acquainted," John grumbles, digging into his heaping plateful of meat and potatoes.

"Your dad is a man of few words," Robin laughs, looking fondly over at John, "Are all you boys the strong and silent types as well?"

I remember the way Cash picked me up in his arms as if it were nothing, last night. Flipping me over, taking me from behind—

"I don't know if I'd put it that way," Luke chuckles, "We all have more than our fair share of differences."

"Sounds like my girls, too," Robin nods, "Annabel takes after me, with her photography and all. Maddie's our little working girl over in Seattle. And Sophia's studying drama and dance at Sheridan University."

"Yeah, I know," Luke replies, as Sophie promptly chokes on her third glass of wine. Or is it her fourth? I've lost count.

"You know what, dear?" Mom asks Luke.

"Luke here is a Sheridan boy too," John says proudly, "Finished undergrad just last year, and he's already back there now for his business degree. They can't get rid of him!"

"Yep. Luke's our college boy," Cash says, none-too-sweetly. "The *only* college boy among the Hawthornes, actually."

"I would have been more than happy to send you to college too," John says gruffly, shooting Cash a look, "You know that full well."

"If I hadn't been wasting my time fighting a war and all?" Cash shoots back.

"You're in the military?" Anna asks, speaking up from her place next to Finn.

"He *was*," Finn replies, ripping a dinner roll in two.

A long, heavy moment of silence swells up, enclosing us all. All four of the Hawthorne men retreat into themselves, leaving us Porter women at a loss. Since no one else is going to, I try my best to dispel the awkwardness.

"So, you and Sophie are at the same school?" I say to Luke. "I'm sure undergrads and graduate students don't see much of each other, though."

"Oh, I think Sophie and I have seen each other around school once or twice," Luke says casually, helping me steer the conversation back toward civility.

That explains why Sophie has been acting so strangely around Luke. Running into a schoolmate in such tight quarters would be pretty awkward. I feel her pain, though I think Cash and I still have the record for strangest origin story so far.

"Sophie, you didn't tell me you knew Luke!" Mom gushes.

"Well, I didn't exactly know we were family friends. Or that I'd be seeing him—*them*—here, did I" Sophie replies shortly, face halfway hidden behind her glass. "Besides, I don't know him. We just go to the same school. With thousands of other people. It's not the same thing."

"I guess Sheridan is a much bigger school than the one me and John met in," Mom laughs, clueless about Sophie's discomfort. "Little Flathead County High was not exactly a hopping place. What did we have, a hundred kids per class?"

"We still had our fun though, didn't we?" John smiles broadly at Mom.

"We sure did," Mom giggles suggestively.

The six of us adult children trade uncomfortable glances across the table. We've been skirting the subject of our parents' relationship, but our questions can't be put off any longer.

"So, what, you two dated in high school or something?" Anna asks.

"Or something…" John replies vaguely.

"Actually," Mom goes on conspiratorially, "John and I were engaged."

Six heads whip around the face the eldest Porter and Hawthorne.

"Well, *that's* a conversation we haven't had," I say tersely.

"You were engaged?" Sophie exclaims, jaw hanging open, "What…When?!"

"All through senior year of high school," Mom says, somewhat wistfully.

"But I couldn't keep this one pinned down in Podunk, Montana," John puts in, with a lingering edge to his voice.

"My scholarship to art school came through, and I couldn't pass it up," Mom sighs, "Besides, we were so young…"

"Isn't art school where you met Dad?" Anna asks pointedly.

"It is," Mom replies, her benign smile faltering for the first time as Dad is invoked.

"So if that scholarship hadn't come through, you would have stayed here and married John…" Anna drives on, her imagination reeling. The rest of us return hastily to our plates of food, feeling none-too-comfortable about this line of questioning.

"That was the plan," John says with a tight smile.

"So if you think about it," Anna continues, looking back at forth between John and our mother, "John is sort of, like, our almost-dad."

I nearly spit out my mouthful of wine at Anna's assessment. God, when you put it like that, my dalliance with Cash suddenly sounds *way* weirder than it has any reason to. If our parents were engaged once, then what does that make us to each other? And why do I suddenly have the incredible urge to crawl under the kitchen table and never emerge?

I'm certainly not the only sibling at the table looking a little squeamish at this little revelation. Sophie is staring intently into her wine glass as Luke shovels food very deliberately into his mouth. Even Cash's face has gone a bit stony—maybe with trying to figure out what this twist means for the two of us.

"Almost-dad," Mom giggles airily, "What a thing to say, Anna! You've always been the inventive one."

"She's got a point though," John shrugs, "There's no way of knowing what might have been, if only…"

"No real need to wonder about what might have been though, is there?" I snap, surprising even myself with my heated tone, "Seeing as we had a dad, and all. A great dad."

"Maddie," Sophie murmurs, trying to staunch my verbal torrent.

"*Had* a dad?" Finn asks from across the table.

"Yeah. Had. He died," I say shortly, "But I guess someone forgot to relay that information, too."

A tense silence comes down hard over the table, and I feel Cash's hazel eyes swing my way. There's a tinge of something like pity in his gaze, and that does me in. All at once, the situation becomes too much for me to handle. Between the revelations about my mom and John Hawthorne's past, my grief at seeing Mom with another man at all, and the intensely confusing feelings I'm having for Cash, I feel like the whole world as I know it is falling away beneath me.

"Excuse me," I mutter, pushing back my chair and rising shakily to my feet. "I just…I don't seem to have much of an appetite."

I turn and hurry away before anyone can see the tears welling up in my eyes. No one says a word to stop me as I dash through the house and out the front door, dewy grass clinging to my ankles as I beat a fast retreat to my car. I plant my hands on the driver's side door, steadying myself against the heaving sobs that threaten to overtake me.

My suitcase is still wedged in the back seat. I could take off now and leave this all behind me, go back to the life I've carved out for myself in Seattle. It may be hectic, thankless, and more than a bit lonely, but at least that life is entirely in my control. If nothing else, I know that my heart will be safe there.

But here among the Hawthorne men? I'm not so sure.

Before my will deserts me, I grab the handle of the car door. But before I can yank it open, a firm, decisive hand lands above mine, keeping the door sealed shut.

"Maddie, wait," Cash says urgently, stepping between me and my getaway car.

"What are you doing?" I ask, my hands balling into anxious fists.

"I'm keeping you from running away, that's what," he says, laying those strong, steadying hands on my shoulders.

"Get out of my way, Cash," I say, gritting my teeth to keep from crying, "Whether or not I run away is *my* call. Not yours."

"I know that," he says fiercely, his eyes fixed on mine, "You have every right to be freaked out about this whole thing. Fuck, you have every right to be pissed as hell at the way it got sprung on us. I know I am. Our parents are a couple of selfish assholes. I'm guessing this isn't news to you. "

"So why don't you leave, too?" I ask him, desperate for some answers that will set this whole thing straight. "It hardly seems like you and John are enjoying your quality time together."

"That's for damn sure," Cash laughs roughly, running his hands slowly down my bare arms. "I don't know why I keep giving in and coming back here at all. He and I are never going to get along. Trust me, if this was any other Hawthorne family reunion, I'd already be hitting the road. But this isn't shaping up to be just any family vacation, is it?"

"What are you saying, Cash?" I demand, goosebumps springing up along my skin as his hands trace down my arms.

"I guess I'm saying that I want more than one night with you, too," he growls, taking my hands in his. "I'm saying that I don't give a fuck about what else is going on in this house as long as you're in it."

"Seriously?" I ask, with a nervous laugh, "You're not the least bit weirded out about the fact that our parents—?"

"I stopped caring about what my father says and does a long time ago," Cash cuts me off, "He doesn't control me anymore, Maddie. My life is my own. So fuck no, I'm not weirded out. And I'm not going to let anything he does stand between me and what I want."

"And what is it you want now?" I ask, my voice barely above a whisper.

I gasp as Cash catches my face in his powerful hands, raising it to his. In answer, he brings his mouth to mine, kissing me hard in the gathering darkness of the night. I let my mouth open to his at once, pressing my body to him as I feel his tongue sweep against mine. We've scarcely known each other a day, but my every nerve is already hard-wired to him. My body comes alive as the taste, the smell, the feel of him envelops me. I feel myself awakening with an urgency that only he can set off.

"I want you to stay, Maddie," he growls, circling my waist with his thickly muscled arms. "I don't want you to disappear from my life just like that."

"But Cash…" I begin, head swimming as I peer up at him in the dark.

"Don't worry about the rest of them," he tells me fiercely, brushing the blonde hair out of my face, "Just answer me honestly: Am I someone you want to know for more than a day?"

"Of course you are," I tell him resolutely.

"Then don't go. Not yet," he says, holding me close as I rest my hands on his firm chest. "Stay, and let me make it worth your while."

I pause, biting my lip. As long as I can remember, I've put my family's needs and desires before my own—especially my mother's. My instinct as a daughter is to get out of her way, let her have this affair with John Hawthorne, even if it only lasts a couple of weeks. Even if it stands between me and the most engaging, sexy, fascinating man I've met in my life. But she's asked me and my sisters here for a reason. I know that deep down, she wants to find a way to have a relationship. And if I'm honest, I want that too. So if I *do* stay, I guess everybody wins…

"Come on," Cash urges, a small smile lifting the corner of his mouth, "Remember how I followed through with the last promise I made you?"

The image of him lowering his mouth to my aching sex comes roaring into my memory. *I'm gonna make you wish for a whole lot more than one night*, he'd told me, before unleashing a torrent of unimaginably wild pleasure inside of me. I feel my thighs clench involuntarily just thinking of it, and know in that moment that I can't deprive myself of this man just yet.

"OK," I whisper, circling my arms around his built shoulders. "I'll stay here with you, Cash. But I'm holding you to that promise."

"You'd better hold on tight, then," he tells me, grin widening.

"Why?" I reply, anticipatory butterflies careening around my stomach, "What have you got in mind for me?"

"You'll see…" he says, grabbing hold of my hips, "You'll see." I let out a laugh as he spins me around, gives me a smack on the ass, and says, "Now march, soldier."

"Yes sir," I reply coyly, relishing the way his eyes skirt down my body as I walk out in front of him. I let my hips sway just a little, and hear Cash groan in response.

"If you're not careful, I'm gonna have to tackle you right here on the front lawn," he warns me, catching up, "What would our dear parents think about that?"

"Do me a favor, Cash," I reply with a shudder, "As long as we're here, don't refer to them as *our* parents, all right? We're toeing the creepy line enough as it is."

"Fair enough, Porter" he laughs, scaling the porch steps in two effortlessly long strides, "Fair enough."

Chapter Six

Over the next few days, the underlying tensions among our mixed-family party begin to die down. Or at least, they dip back beneath the surface for the time being. Everyone seems able to relax into the spirit of vacation, spending their days as they wish while giving each other plenty of room. Each of us falls into our own routine, coming together maybe once a day to check in. The less time we all spend in the same room, it seems, the better things tend to go.

But then, it's not like familial tension is new to either of the present families. The relationship between us Porter girls and our mother is rightfully strained. Despite her imaginative and expressive personality, her tendency to be flighty, absent-minded, and self-absorbed have made her a less than ideal mother, at times. I know that no one's perfect, and I don't expect her to be either. But her shortcomings have stunted her daughters' ability to trust and rely on her, especially when we've needed it most. I know I'll keep trying my entire life to have a relationship with her, but so far, it hasn't gotten any easier.

What's interesting, though, is that there seems to be a very similar coldness to the Hawthorne boys' relationships with John. Luke seems the most determined to keep things civil, but he treats his dad with more respect than affection. Finn, the youngest, seems to have pulled an Annabel and fostered a self-sufficiency that makes a relationship with his dad all but unnecessary. Of all three brothers, Cash seems to be the one who butts heads with his dad the most fiercely. There's a bitterness to their fighting that tells of deep, unresolved strife.

But seeing as Cash Hawthorne isn't exactly a "talk about your feelings" kind of guy, I'm pretty in the dark about his family's past. I don't know anything about the circumstances of his enlisting in the army, or what's beneath the rivalry he has with Luke, or even what the story is with his absent mother. Maybe I'll find out in time, though I get the feeling that Cash's emotional side isn't going to be an easy nut to crack.

Despite his persuasive promises to make staying here at the lake house worth my while, Cash plays a very cool game with me as the first week wears on. Though we seemed to end up alone at every turn that first day, it's not a pattern that holds. Sure, I see enough of him—I just never quite catch him alone. Around the house, down by the lake, and even on some excursions into the woods, there's always someone else keeping us from getting some alone time. He doesn't seem too perturbed by the constant company—I wonder if he's letting me squirm like this on purpose? Trying to build up the anticipation or something?

Whatever the plan is, I hope this phase of it is over soon. I can't go much longer without another taste of him.

One afternoon halfway through the week, I find myself lounging on the dock with Anna and Sophie, catching some much-needed rays. My office-bound body is super pale, even compared to my similarly fair-skinned sisters. I'm rocking my favorite bikini— a red bandeau top with matching bottoms—and have my hair pulled up into a white bandana, Rosie the Riveter style. Sophie's wearing a super skimpy black bikini and huge Jackie O sunglasses, her long caramel hair woven into a mermaid tail braid. Anna's classic white halter top bathing suit complements her nearly platinum locks, which hang loose over her freckled shoulders. It's a rare event indeed that all three Porter sisters are in the same place (and good spirits) long enough to have a good old fashioned gab session, but that's exactly what we're up to now.

"I give you a lot of credit," I tell Anna, letting my toes dangle in the cool lake water, "I wouldn't have had the wherewithal to take a gap year before college at your age."

"Well, you knew what you wanted to go to school for," my little sister shrugs, lying on her stomach beside me, "I'm still feeling it out."

"I just couldn't wait to get out of the house," Sophie puts in, "Don't get me wrong, I love my program at

Sheridan. But more than anything, getting away from Mom was the priority."

"Yeah, well. Imagine being the only one in the house with her after Dad died," Anna says with a rare hint of condemnation.

Sophie and I exchange an uneasy look. Anna was only sixteen when Dad was killed. With me away at school already and Sophie on the cusp of leaving, Anna was on her own with Mom in the aftermath of the accident. As flaky and distant as our Mom was at the best of times, Anna's experience with her in the throes of grief was on a whole different level. In a lot of ways, our youngest sister had to finish raising herself on her own. And it shows, too. She's far more mature than Sophie and I were at her age…Or even now, for that matter.

Now that I think of it, I think that Anna's even-keeled nature is the trait she most clearly inherited from our dad. Archie Porter was entirely unflappable, utterly dependable, and straightforward at all times. He never lied to us, even when we were little girls. I remember him that way—with his lean, long-limbed body, sandy hair, and horn rimmed glasses—laying his hands on my shoulders and giving it to me straight. I may have gotten his love of literature and learning, but Annabel absolutely got his insistence on telling the truth—whether or not anyone wants to hear it.

"So, uh…have you given any thought to how you'll spend the year?" I ask Anna, somewhat awkwardly changing the subject.

"Mostly just building up my photography portfolio," she replies, rolling onto her back on the warm deck boards. "I want to get some more portraits and event photography."

"I could hire you for the next ReImaged party!" I offer enthusiastically. It's not often that Anna's world and mine intersect, and I can't help but leap at the opportunity.

"Yeah, maybe," she replies noncommittally, puncturing the bubble of my excitement, "I was thinking of heading in a less corporate direction, though. Finn's letting me tag along to his band's show tonight to take some shots of them, actually."

"Finn's in a band?!" Sophie exclaims, sitting bolt upright.

"Yeah. He's the lead vocalist," Anna replies placidly.

"But I've barely heard a full sentence out of him," I say incredulously. I can't deny that I feel a little pang of jealousy that Finn's work is more interesting to Anna than mine.

"Yeah. I didn't realize he spoke in full sentences," Sophie adds.

"Maybe that's because neither of you lets anyone else get a word in. Ever think of that?" Anna shoots back, that hint of heat rising into her usually cool voice once more.

"Whoa, Anna…" Sophie replies, stung. "That's a little harsh."

"Yeah, well. The truth can be a bitch," Anna shrugs, pulling herself to her feet.

"Did we do something wrong?" I ask my little sister as she gathers her things, "You seem really pissed off at us."

Anna levels her gold-flecked eyes at me, with a frankness that reaches down to the corners of my soul.

"I just wish the two of you would think about someone besides yourselves once in a while," she says, swinging her gaze between me and Sophie. She doesn't sound angry, or even sad—just terribly disappointed. It's the sort of tone that makes you feel about two inches tall, especially when it's coming from someone who's supposed to look up to you.

"Anna, what are you talking about?" Sophie asks her, looking as wary as I feel.

"Come on," Anna says, shaking her head, "You can't play dumb with me, you guys. I know you too well for that."

Before we can utter another word, Anna turns on her heel and marches away. As she goes, a knot of unease twists in my stomach. What have I done to make her so upset? Could it be possible that she's somehow caught wind of what's going on between me and Cash? She's always been crazy perceptive, and that would certainly explain her disapproval of me. But then what the hell could she have on Sophie?

"Do you have any idea what she's on about?" I ask Sophie, trying to keep my voice light.

"Nope," Sophie replies, a little too quickly. "No idea."

"Huh. You know Anna. Always the sensitive one," I offer, convincing no one. "We should probably just let her go off and do her own thing. Close quarters do weird things to people…"

Sophie and I fall into an uneasy silence, angling our bodies away from each other. Try as I might, I can't think of anything neutral to say to her. We've already burned through all our small talk about work and school, and the only thing we seem to have in common these days is our dysfunctional family.

What I wouldn't give to have that closeness the three of us shared as little girls. I remember being nine years old, with six-year-old Sophie and four-year-old Anna, living on our sprawling farm in Vermont. We'd roam that land for hours on end, making up games and languages, sharing stories and secrets. Three tow-headed, rough-and-tumble girls, united in the kind of love that only sisters can know. God, how I mourn the loss of that closeness. Though this is the first time in a long while that all three of us Porter sisters have been in the same place, I've never felt further away from them both.

A flash of bright red catches my eye up by the house. As I turn to get a closer look, my eyes land squarely on the fine, perfectly balanced form that's occupied my every waking daydream these past few days—that of Cash Hawthorne, of course. And a *shirtless* Cash Hawthorne, nonetheless.

His defined pecs and gloriously cut abs are getting tanner by the day, here by the lake. He's got one end of a red kayak balanced on his shoulder, holding it up effortlessly with his thick, powerful arms. His long dark curls are pushed back from his sculpted face, and his light blue jeans are riding low on the muscular "V" of his hips. So entranced am I by the sight of my tatted up, scruffy paramour that I barely notice Luke holding up the other end of the kayak. When it comes to the Hawthorne brothers, I can't help playing favorites.

"Jesus Christ," Cash crows, trundling toward us with the kayak in tow. "I should have worn some shades down here—that pale ass skin of yours is gonna make me go blind."

"Ha, ha," Sophie replies, tossing her long braid over her shoulder, "Just wait until you're an old, sunbaked, wrinkly dude at the age of thirty, and then we'll see who's laughing."

"He's already a grumpy old asshole on the inside," Luke puts in as the guys lower the kayak onto the dock, "I'm sure the outside will match before long."

Sophie zips her lips the second Luke jumps into the conversation, turning back toward the lake. What the hell is the deal with these two? Luke must have seen her pull a *Girls Gone Wild* at a college party or something, for all the tension that seems to hang between them. Hell, maybe there was even some kind of ill-advised hookup back at Sheridan. That would certainly explain things. Though the chances of two Porter-Hawthorne hookups—make that *three*, including our parents—seem pretty slim.

"You got the keys to the truck?" Cash asks Luke, brushing off his hands.

"What do you need it for?" Luke replies, handing Cash a set of keys to the ancient black pickup truck that lives on the property.

"Need some more smokes," Cash says, laughing at the grimace that crosses Luke's face. "Sack up, man. It's not meth."

"Oh, right. I forgot that lung cancer is real fucking manly," Luke shoots back. "Forget sacking up—when are you gonna try *growing* up, Cash?"

"What would I do that for?" Cash shrugs, "You're already playing man of the house around here, isn't that right little brother?"

"I'm not *playing* at anything, you fucker," Luke snaps back, squaring off against Cash, "All I'm doing is picking up your slack."

"What a good little boy," Cash grins, punching Luke in the shoulder—just hard enough for it not to be a joke.

"Don't touch me, asshole," Luke spits, his hands balling into fists.

"Come on, lil' guy," Cash eggs Luke on, giving him a firm shove, "You still afraid to take on your big, bad brother?"

Sophie and I exchange nervous glances as Luke's eyes flare with anger.

"I've always preferred fair fights, Cash. *Clean* fights," Luke shoots back at his brother, "Not exactly your specialty."

I watch Cash's jaw pulse with rage as Luke's barb catches him. It's the same look that came over John yesterday, while he and Cash were on the verge of fighting. For all their differences, it looks like there's one thing Cash inherited from his father—a willingness to fight, and fight *hard*. Though maybe this wasn't so much inherited as beaten into him. My heart aches, just thinking about what might have befallen these boys when they were small.

"Guys, come on. Chill out..." I say, rising to my feet as the Hawthorne brothers face off on the dock.

"Seriously, you're being idiots," Sophie adds, hurrying to stand beside me.

"You girls just aren't used to the way guys settle things," Cash smiles coldly, his eyes fixed hard on Luke.

"The way *some* guys settle things," Luke corrects him, lifting his chin defiantly, "No matter the consequences. Right, Cash?"

All at once, the playfulness goes out of Cash's eyes. His gaze becomes steely, that sharp jaw pulsing even harder with raw anger.

"Cash…" I say warily, taking a step toward them, "Could you please just drop this? You're freaking me out."

"Yeah Luke," Sophie adds, joining me as I inch forward to diffuse the brewing fist fight, "This is nuts. You guys are brothers."

"In name, maybe," Luke growls, looking at Cash with pure contempt, "But thankfully, that's all."

"That's the good ol' Hawthorne name for you," Cash grins, pulling himself back from the brink of losing it, with nothing short of Herculean effort, "It'll stick to you like a motherfucker, even if it doesn't mean shit."

Luke turns away from Cash, looking for the world like his brother's just spat in his face. There's a bad streak in the blood these brothers share—and I'm starting to get the feeling that it runs very, very deep.

"Well," Cash goes on, his ripped body still humming in the wake of the barely-avoided brawl, "I'm off. You wanna ride with?"

My heart thrills for just a second at his offer…until I see that I'm not the one he's extended it to. Instead, his eyes are fixed on Sophie, who looks just as surprised as I feel—though not as gutted, I'm sure.

"Oh. Uh…OK," she says uncertainly, her eyes darting first toward Luke, then toward me. "Yeah, why not. I haven't really seen much of the town here."

"Great," Cash replies, nodding at the truck waiting in the long driveway, "Though fair warning, there's not much of a town to see. It's kind of a shit hole, to be honest."

"Well, now I *have* to see it," Sophie laughs, following Cash up the dock.

I stand on the gently swaying boards, watching the two of them walking away together. It's a perfectly innocuous outing, not the least bit charged—so then why do I feel like I've been slapped in the face?

"I didn't know those two, uh, got along so well…" I say to Luke, my voice hollow.

"Mhm," he grunts back, his jaw clamped shut. He stares as Cash leads Sophie to the pickup, and tries in vain not to look furious. He doesn't seem too thrilled about their little adventure, either.

"But *you* and Sophie," I bait him, taking full advantage of his distracted state, "You two already have a history…"

"What?" he snaps, whipping around to face me.

"You know each other from school, I mean," I go on. Looks like I've hit a nerve, here. And not a very concealed one, either.

"Right," Luke replies, shoving his hands into the pockets of his jeans.

He's gone shirtless this afternoon, as well. His body is just as sculpted as Cash's, though without the ink and occasional scar. But whereas Cash's body seems to have been built up from combat, boxing, and MMA brawls, Luke's is more finely honed. He's an athlete and a Crossfit buff, I've learned. A star runner for the Sheridan track team, when he was an undergrad. In fact, that's how he earned his scholarship there. When my artsy sister would have ever been in the same room as a jock is beyond me, though…

"How did you guys meet? At school?" I decide to press him, sitting back down at the edge of the dock.

"She never mentioned?" he asks, moving to stand beside me. I sense a note of disappointment in his voice.

"Nope. We don't really talk much, on a regular basis," I inform him, letting my feet dangle into the water.

"Huh," he says, crossing his arms.

"So, do you guys have mutual friends, or…?" I prod.

"Actually," he says, looking down at me, "I was her teacher. Well, TA."

My jaw falls open as I absorb this information. "You were her teacher's assistant?" I ask him, agog.

"That's right," he replies. "Don't look so shocked. Not all the Hawthorne men are hulked-out neanderthals like my dear big brother."

"It's just…That's not what I was imagining…" I reply, shaking my head, "About how you guys met, I mean."

"What exactly *were* you imagining?" he asks, a slow grin creeping across his face.

"I'm sure you can guess," I say, smiling back.

"Not too hard to," he laughs, rolling his eyes, "But you're way off. Sophie was in the econ class I was assisting last semester.

"Then why haven't you mentioned that to anyone here?" I ask him. "Sounds to me like you're hiding something…"

"I'm not hiding anything," he shrugs, "TAs only have a couple one-on-one meetings with their students during the semester. I just graded a couple of her papers. That's it."

"You sure that's not a euphemism for something?" I tease him.

"Christ. Someone's got a one-track mind," he replies, nudging me with his foot.

"You didn't answer the question," I remind him, enjoying the camaraderie despite myself.

"You Porter women are relentless, aren't you?" he says, "I don't know which one of you is the most stubborn."

"It's a four way tie," I say lightly.

"Sounds familiar," he replies.

A silence unfolds between us, the jocular mood fading away as we hear the pickup truck start with a wheeze and take off down the driveway. It's ridiculous to be jealous of Sophie for getting some alone time with Cash; ridiculous to be suspicious of his motives for taking her on a little joy ride…yet here I am, all jealousy and suspicion. What a charming combination.

"I'm gonna take this thing out," Luke says tersely, walking over to the single-seat kayak and lowering himself in. "Enjoy the peace and quiet."

"Thanks," I say wistfully, drawing my knees into my chest.

Luke grabs the paddle and pushes himself away from the dock. He chops at the water with strong, determined strokes, and soon he's disappeared from sight around an outcropping of trees. For perhaps the first time since arriving here at the lake house, I'm all alone.

I should be used to the feeling by now, having spent much of these past few years by myself in tiny apartments, tiny cubicles, the private world of my own grief that opened wide within my tiny self after Dad died. But, surrounded by all this huge open space, my own loneliness is amplified tenfold. Sitting beside the expansive waters of the lake, underneath the arching sky, among ancient rocks and trees…I feel smaller than ever. More alone than ever. But even so, I realize there's only one person who could fill the massive void of my lonesomeness. And my little sister is currently riding shotgun in his truck.

Perfect. Just *perfect*.

Chapter Seven

I retire to my bedroom absurdly early that night, claiming to have a headache. What's truly aching is that bruised, beating muscle in my chest, but no one else needs to know that. This little vacation is almost halfway over, so why do I feel more tense and exhausted than when I arrived? I lay wide awake in my guest room as the hours slip by, and before I know it the night is nearly over, without my having slept a wink. What I wouldn't give for a little stress relief of the kind Cash and I enjoyed that first night at the motel…

Despite his avowed pledge to "make my stay worthwhile", I've barely seen hide or hair of Cash since that first night we spent here. And trust me, I'd like to see all of that hide if I could get another chance. He said himself that he doesn't give a shit about what our parents' relationship is, so what the hell gives? Did he just lose interest in me overnight? I decide to consult the expert on all matters concerning my love life. In other words, I give Allie a call.

"MaddieMaddieMaddie!" she squeals upon picking up.

"What're you, happy to hear from me or something?" I ask, flopping down onto the guest room's twin bed.

"Just a little," she replies.

"I hope I didn't call too late," I go on, glancing at the digital clock pulsing 3:00am in big red digits. "I was really just going to leave you a message…"

"It's never too late for my best friend," she says cheerfully. I hear a far less perky, very distinctly male voice grumble in the background, despite Allie's shushing.

"Got a visitor?" I ask.

"Something like that," she replies. "Brian. Or…Ryan? I don't remember. He just went to get a glass of water, so I can't even fact check…"

"God, I've missed you," I laugh.

"What, haven't you had a slew of hookups since you broke the seal a couple nights back?" she asks mischievously. "I still can't believe my little Maddie is all grown up and screwing random hotties in motels…"

"Just the one hottie," I reminder her, rolling onto my side, "And, uh…Not so random either, it turns out."

"Excuse me. What does *that* mean?" Allie demands.

I bite my lip—an impressive feat, given how far my foot is jammed into my mouth. I'm torn between wanting to tell Allie everything about Cash and wanting to give her as few details as possible. She was more than supportive of my sexy one night stand, but what if she's weirded out by what's come after? It doesn't bother me that John Hawthorne and my mom are…whatever they are to each other, but I can't count on anyone else feeling the same way, even if that someone is Allie. I may just have to get a little…creative with the details.

"You'll never believe it," I laugh dryly, "But the guy I slept with that first night? The one I sent you a picture of? He's…uh…a *local*."

"Get out," Allie breathes. I can practically hear her big green eyes widening into dinner plates. "He lives in that middle-of-nowhere town you're staying with your family?"

"He does, yeah," I tell her—not exactly a lie. "I've even bumped into him a few times," also, more true than not.

"Has anything else happened with him?" Allie asks breathlessly.

"There was another kiss," I allow, my entire body recalling how it feels to lock lips with Cash Hawthorne, "But nothing else so far."

"What the hell are you waiting for?" Allie laughs, "Go jump those country boy bones while you still can!"

"What about our little bet?" I challenge her, "It won't really have been a one night stand if I sleep with him again, right?"

"Do you honestly think I give a single shit about that stupid bet when the best sex of your life in on the line?!" Allie all but screeches. "What kind of a shitty friend do you think I am?"

"So I take it I have your blessing, then?" I laugh.

"You have *all* of my blessings. Every last one," she tells me, "Who knows? Maybe this one night stand of yours could turn into your first relationship with a guy that actually turns you on. At all."

"What a novel idea," I say sarcastically. But her suggestion sticks in my heart. I've hardly dared to let myself think the word *relationship* since meeting Cash Hawthorne. It doesn't even seem to exist in the same universe as him. That's the main reason I didn't insist on the two of us just leaving this place together and carrying out our little affair somewhere else. If we were to continue things outside of this place, we'd be risking rushing into some kind of relationship. And knowing me, I'd mess it up immediately. As long as we stay here, united by coincidence, there's far less pressure. Cash hardly seems like a relationship sort of guy. But if I've learned one thing this week, it's that anything is possible…why not Cash and I as a pair?

If he hasn't already staked his claim on another Porter sister, that is.

A soft, rhythmic tapping catches my ear as Allie mutters something to Brian-or-Ryan. This big rustic house has a vocabulary of taps, clangs, and stirrings all its own. I've been told to ignore them, but as this new tapping reasserts itself, I sit up in my modest twin bed. My heart starts hammering in my ears, much more loudly than the noise that's set it off.

Someone's knocking at my bedroom door.

"Allie, hold on," I whisper into the receiver, swinging my legs over the side of my bed.

"What's happening?" I hear my best friend say as I make my way across the room.

With my heart lodged firmly in my throat, I twist the handle and pull the door open an inch. The warm light from my bedside lamp falls through the narrow opening, illuminating a vibrant set of very familiar hazel eyes.

"Maddie, are you OK?" Allie's tinny voice asks as I stare up at my early-morning visitor.

"I have to call you back," I mutter faintly into the phone, hanging up abruptly as Cash pushes the door open to reveal himself.

"Fancy meeting you here," Cash grins his voice hushed. He leans against the doorway and letting his eyes travel up and down my scantly-clad body. I'm suddenly very aware of how tiny my cotton shorts and tank top really are, and cross my arms compulsively over my chest.

"What do you want, Cash?" I whisper, though my every nerve rallies at the sight of him.

"What's with the attitude?" he asks, cocking his head. A single curl falls across his forehead, and I have to force myself to keep taking deep breaths.

"It's three in the morning," I inform him, "Normal people are asleep at this hour."

"And yet, here we are," he smiles, taking a step toward me.

Apprehension and anticipation war for control of my body. This is the first time Cash and I have been alone since our sultry kiss the other night. But we're also surrounded by several sleeping family members who could discover us at any minute. I may have only spent one night with Cash, but I know that I can't keep quiet once his hands are on me.

"You shouldn't be here," I tell him. "It's not...You know..."

"What?" he asks, laying his hands on my bare arms, "*Proper*?"

"Fuck proper," I snap, "It's just not cool of you, Cash. You've been straight up ignoring me ever since the first night we got here. You can't just stroll on into my room and expect a booty call after—"

"Whoa, whoa," Cash says, holding me fast, "Slow down, Maddie. What do you mean I've been ignoring you?"

I stare at him, unspeaking. Cash Hawthorne may be handsome as hell, but he is mighty slow on the uptake.

"You've barely said a word to me in the past few days," I spell it out for him, "You keep avoiding being alone with me, or even being in the same room with me. And this afternoon, you just ran off with Sophie—"

"Well yeah," he says, still not seeing the problem.

"Well *yeah*," I echo, trying to ignore the warmth of his hands against my skin.

"Maddie, I've been making sure to throw the rest of them off our trail," he tells me, as if *I'm* the crazy one.

"…What?" I ask faintly.

"I mean, I don't give a shit about what our families think, but I still don't want them all over us, you know?" he says, running his hands down my arms, "Playing it like we're not cool, taking Sophie out for a drive, it was all just the scramble the signal. You didn't think I'd actually lost interest or whatever, did you?"

"I…No…" I lie, badly as ever. I feel a hot blush rising to my cheeks, which only grows in intensity the longer Cash's hazel eyes linger on my face.

"You're adorable when you're bullshitting," he grins at me, circling my slender waist with his inked arms.

"Shut up," I mutter, though I can't keep my face from breaking into a smile.

"There it is," he murmurs, pulling me to him. Instinctively, I lace my arms around his neck. It's crazy how familiar his body already feels against mine.

"You couldn't have just told me what you were up to?" I chide him gently.

"I don't know if you've figured this out yet," he says, raising an eyebrow, "But the whole *explaining myself* thing isn't really for me."

"You don't say," I laugh softly, savoring the feel of his hard body against mine. As my apprehensions fall away, my body rises with renewed want of him. I'm keenly aware of the twin bed, standing just paces away from us. What I wouldn't give to be bent over that thing, with Cash poised over me—

"Come on," he says, cutting off my steamy train of thought. He takes my hand in his and tugs me toward the door, "Let's go."

"G-go?" I splutter, digging my heels into the hardwood floor, "Go where?"

"What's the matter?" Cash grins, looking at me over his broad shoulder, "You scared of a little adventure, Porter?"

There it is again: a challenge I can't refuse. I have no idea what Cash has in store for us, but I can't very well back down now.

"Of course not," I tell him, playing it cool, "Lead the way."

We pad through the enormous, slumbering home, silencing our footfalls as best we can at this early hour. I'm convinced that the loudest noise on hand is my wrecking ball of a heart, but still we make it out of the house undetected. Cash leads me out through the kitchen door, onto the dew-slicked patio. A nearly full moon hangs in the sky over the lake, lighting our path across the sprawling back lawn down toward the lake. A million stars career overhead in a dizzying canopy, and I almost lose my footing trying to take them all in. Luckily, I have Cash's hand to steady me.

"This place is amazing," I whisper, as we step out onto the darkened dock. "I can't believe you got to grow up here."

"Yeah," he allows, letting his gaze follow mine up to the heavens, "As bad as things ever got, at least I always had this."

"Did things get…really bad?" I ask tentatively, as Cash draws me along the planks.

He doesn't answer me for a long moment. I can sense that we've reached the threshold of what most people know about him. What he ever dares to confide in another person. I can feel the massive effort it takes for him to continue, see it in his very bearing.

"They did," he finally says, drawing to a stop before me. "I'd feel fucking stupid complaining about it, with what happened to your family—"

"Don't," I tell him, resting my hands on his tapered waist, "There are different kinds of bad. I know that."

Cash draws a deep breath, bracing himself. "Well. We sort of lost our mom, too. Only, not to any freak accident or illness or whatever. Just…because that's what she decided she wanted. She bailed on us when we were kids. Didn't dig the whole 'cabin in the woods' vibe my dad set up. Wanted more *things*. More money. Joke was on her, though—Dad's business took off right after she hit the road. He built this place, let the three of us run wild all over it, just us guys…"

I hold my tongue as he goes on. Suddenly, the Hawthorne boys' aversion to female company is starting to make sense.

"She's living on the East Coast now. Boston. Married some real slick lawyer type and popped out another couple kids with him. Girls, like she always wanted. They're teenagers, by now. And hopefully giving her all kinds of hell."

"I grew up in a family with three girls who were all teenagers at the same time," I remind him, "Trust me, your mom had her hands full."

"Shit, listen to me…" Cash mutters, laughing roughly, "Spilling my guts like—"

"I want to know these things about you, Cash," I assure him, circling his waist, "If you'll let me listen…you can spill your guts all night."

"Fine," he says, with a crooked grin, "But I'm not doing it on dry land."

"What…?" I ask, as he tugs me toward the edge of the dock.

Bobbing on the water is a long wooden canoe, with benches for two. The boys must have moved it down to the water with the kayaks this afternoon. And from the look on Cash's face, I imagine this is what he had in mind all the while.

My handsome companion hops down into the sleek vessel, offering up his hand to help me in. I'm far more nervous than I have any cause to be. Is it the glassy black waters of the lake that has my heart racing? Or the depth of what Cash is revealing to me about himself? Or simply the fact of being close to him, out there where no one is bound to stumble upon us…

"You coming or what?" Cash asks me, his bright smile shining in the blackness of the early morning.

"You're damn right I am," I breathe, grabbing hold of his firm, strong hand and stepping down into the canoe.

Chapter Eight

The vessel parts the water's surface like silk as we coast along in the moonlight. Cash's powerful arms work the oars, propelling us easily toward our destination—whatever that might be. The exertion distracts him, gives him an outlet as he tells me more about the life that's led him to this moment.

"Dad wanted me to go to college more than anything," he says, pulling the heavy wooden oars along another arc, "His plan was for me to take over the contracting business, as the oldest son and all. But I could never picture myself wasting four years of my life that way. I thought, it was easy for him to want that for me—he'd never been through it himself. There was no way I was going to do what he wanted, but I don't think either of us could have known how far I'd blow by the mark…"

"By joining the army instead?" I ask gently.

"Exactly," Cash goes on, "It was the last thing Dad wanted for me. He already felt he'd lost part of his family when Mom left. He thought it was my responsibility to stay and oversee things. But when I looked at the state of the world, then…Everything that had happened to our country, in the Middle East, far beyond our little lakeside bubble…I knew I couldn't just plant my feet and stay here. I needed to see what could be done. What *I* could do. Guess I thought I was real hot shit when I was eighteen, imagining I could go off and save the world."

"Were you…Did you…" I stammer, unsure of how to proceed.

"You want to know about my time in the Army?" Cash asks, "There's not a whole lot to tell, to be honest."

"Somehow, I find that hard to believe," I reply.

He gives a wry laugh. "I just mean, I wasn't there for long. Truth be told, I'd barely seen combat when I was discharged."

"Were you injured?"

"That I was," he says, his eyes hardening, "But not like you might imagine."

"You don't have to tell me," I say softly, resting a hand on Cash's knee, "But you can. If you like…"

For the first time since setting out, he brings his muscled arms to a stop. The constant, lulling sound of the oar stokes dies away as we coast along the clear lake in silence. In this moment, it feels like we're the only two people in the world, that nothing this remarkable has ever happened to anyone before. I take in the sight of Cash, his profile cutting a sharp line against the backdrop of the lake, and know that I'll remember this moment for as long as I live, whatever becomes of us now.

"I was injured," he says slowly, his eyes cast off across the lake, "But not in combat with the enemy. In a fight that broke out in our quarters. A fight I started to…because I…"

He speaks through gritted teeth, fighting for every word he manages to spit out. I get the feeling he's never talked to anyone about this—at least not in a very long time.

"What was the fight about, Cash?" I ask quietly, my near-whisper carrying out across the still lake.

Cash draws a deep breath into his lungs and levels those intense hazel eyes on me.

"There was this guy in my unit. An asshole jock type named Rick. He was one of those guys who ruled his hometown, a real golden boy prick. Thought he was entitled to anything he wanted 'cause no one had been able to take him down before.

"Rick and I were stationed in Iraq together. Us and a handful of other young new recruits. There was one guy in particular who seemed younger than all the rest of us—Drew. Really quiet, great with computers, played the guitar. He reminded me a lot of Finn…This was back when Finn was still fourteen, before he shot up like a damn weed.

"Anyway, we all got our asses handed to us the first couple months in Iraq. Training is one thing, but nothing can prepare you for being over there. You're always on guard. One false move and you're done.

And it's not just the stress of constant danger, it's fucking *lonely*. Not to mention that with a bunch of young guys spending every waking moment together, there's gonna be some fucked up power plays and shit going on. Rick was the worst with that. Always trying to one-up the rest of us, prove that he was invincible…"

"Is that how your fight started?" I ask Cash, "Some sort of power struggle with this guy?"

"I wish that was it," Cash says, shaking his head. For the first time since I've known him, I hear sadness color his voice. Regret.

"Then…what?" I press.

"I told you that Rick was a guy who went after whatever he wanted," Cash says, tearing his eyes away from mine. "I could look the other way as long as what he wanted was the best bunk, or the most high-profile mission, or even first dibs on grub. But a couple months into our tour…he decided that what he wanted was a little human *contact*. And since our base wasn't exactly crawling with ladies…he decided he wanted it from the one person on hand who couldn't fight back. He decided to go after Drew."

My stomach turns over as I come to understand Cash's meaning.

"Holy shit," I whisper, feeling the color drain from my face.

"Yeah, holy shit," Cash growls, remembering. "People are only just starting to realize how many women get assaulted while serving. But the men? It happens to more of them than you'd ever believe, and they're even less likely to talk about it. I had no idea going into the Army that this kind of thing could happen. I was so fucking naive. It happens all the goddamn time. It happened…on my watch.

"I picked up on Rick's motives early on, the way he'd tear Drew down around the rest of us, try and make him feel powerless. I started keeping an eye on Drew on the sly—we were nearly the same age, but he still felt like a kid brother to me. I had to let him out of my sight for a few hours one night while I was on patrol, but the second I got back I knew something was up. Rick and Drew were nowhere to be seen, and the rest of the guys were barely speaking. Everyone knew what was going on, but no one was going to stop it. Maybe they thought—hey, better him than me.

"I found the two of them in one of the deserted bunks. Rick had Drew cornered, pinned up against the wall, and…I don't want to upset you with a play-by-play. I'll never forget that moment. It wasn't just feeling terrible for Drew, it was knowing that we'd all failed to protect him—*I'd* failed."

"It sounds like you were the only one who *didn't* fail him, Cash," I say, tears pricking my eyes at the thought of Drew. Of all the other guys who suffer this same torment in silence. "And it shouldn't have fallen to you, to save him."

"But it did. I completely blacked out," Cash goes on, "The next thing I remember, I'm pounding the shit out of Rick while the rest of the guys try to pull me off. I did a fucking number on him, but I didn't come out totally unscathed. Couple broken ribs. Fucker even pulled his knife on me—he'd already been using it to keep Drew quiet…Long story short, we were both discharged. *Dishonorably* discharged."

"But…but that's such bullshit," I seethe, "You deserve a medal for what you did, not—"

"I don't, is the thing," Cash cuts me off, "What I did for Drew was basic human decency. That's it."

"You don't have to downplay it," I tell him, studying his stony face, his pained eyes.

"To tell you the truth, Maddie…" Cash goes on, reaching for my hand, "That's all I've ever been able to do. When I got kicked out of the Army, all I told people was that I'd gotten in a fight. I couldn't tell them about why the fight had really started—Drew had already been through enough without my using the worst moment of his life to get people off my case."

"You mean…*no one* knows the truth?" I ask, astounded.

"No one but you," he says, rubbing his thumb against my hand. "And a couple of Army shrinks, but—"

"Not your brothers?" I press, "Not even your dad?"

"No," he murmurs, closing his fingers tightly around mine, "*Especially* not my dad. If I'd told him why I'd gotten in that fight, he would have just told me that I should've minded my own business. Kept in line. He'd never understand. He's never understood anything about protecting your own. But you, Porter…Something tells me that you're the only person who could ever understand this. About me."

"I do, Cash," I whisper, staring deeply into his troubled eyes, "Truly, I do."

"Then I hope you also understand," he says, his voice rasping, "That when I care about someone, I'd do fucking anything for them. No matter what the risks. No matter what the consequences. Nothing can stop me from doing right by the people I care for. The *person* I care for. You understand what I'm saying, don't you?"

"I think I do," I whisper back, my heart threatening to burst straight through my ribcage.

"Think?" Cash growls, "I need you to *know*…"

I gasp as Cash wraps his arms around me, scooping me up as if I weighed nothing. He pulls me into his lap as I clasp my hands behind his neck. Brushing the dark blonde hair out of my face, Cash pulls me flush against him, bringing his mouth to mine. I open to him at once, trembling at the passion, the ferocity rippling beneath his muscled surface. Cash works my mouth open wide, letting his tongue sweep powerfully against mine. I swing my legs around, hooking my ankles behind his back and straddling him right there on the canoe bench.

A low growl vibrates from him core as I grind my hips against his already-stiff cock. Cash grabs hold of my ass with both hands, squeezing hard. He pulls me even tighter to that irresistible length, pressing hard in the exact place I need to feel him… *All* of him.

"I love how much you want me," Cash growls, running his hands up along my back.

"Looks like I'm not the only one," I breathe, pressing back against his rigid manhood, "Or should I say, *feels* like…"

"Believe it or not," Cash laughs roughly, drawing back to take me in, "Fucking you dirty in this boat was *not* my plan."

"I don't believe you," I tease, raking my fingers down his chest.

"If you can wait just a little while longer," he says, "I'll show you what I actually had in mind for us."

"You expect me to *wait*?!" I laugh incredulously, "What kind of cruel and unusual—"

"I promise it'll be worth it," he smiles, circling his strong hands around my waist.

"You and your promises…" I murmur, wanting nothing more than to feel him *now*.

"I always make good on them in the end, don't I?" he challenges me. "Come on. Be a good little girl and keep your hands to yourself for just—"

"Call me 'little girl' again and I'm swimming back to shore," I warn him, picking myself up off his lap and making a big show of folding my hands in my lap. It's a bluff, of course. There's no way I could tear myself away from him now. I try to ignore the throbbing need that rings out just beneath them, pounding insistently between my legs.

"Duly noted," Cash grins, grabbing hold of the oars once more.

In a silence pulsing with desperate need, we soar across the lake. I barely notice as the sky loses its inky black sheen, giving way to a rich charcoal, then a heather gray. The sun must be about to rise. I can't think of a better way to greet a new day than this, all alone at the edge of the world with the man I… The man I *what*? Want, certainly. Need, perhaps. But what else?

Do I even dare put a word to how I feel for him?

"Here," Cash says, his voice a low rasp.

I look past the bow of the canoe and spot a small stretch of shoreline. It's entirely hidden from sight, this spot—obscured by overhanging trees and deep woods on all sides. The narrow beach looks unreachable, remote, and entirely private. A kick drum of anticipation starts up in my core as we glide toward the shore. In one masterful motion, Cash swings his legs into the shallow water, towing us the rest of the way. My knees are trembling by the time we've reached the shore. I'm sure that the very edges of my form must be vibrating with barely contained desire.

From under his seat, Cash produces a thick gray blanket, tightly rolled. Tucking it under his arm, he extends his hand to me. I lace my fingers through his, pulling myself to standing. At once, Cash feels my shakiness, and stops to steady me.

"Are you OK?" he asks, training his gaze on me.

"Of course," I smile gamely, willing myself to calm down.

"You're shaking like a leaf," he murmurs, concerned.

"It's nothing," I tell him, laying my hands on his firm chest, "Just…a little overwhelmed, I guess."

His brow furrows. "Did I do something wrong?" he asks, "I didn't mean to scare you with all that—"

"No, Cash…" I cut him off earnestly, "You didn't scare me."

Cash's story of valor and sacrifice didn't scare me in the slightest. Nor did knowing what he's capable of doing, when pushed. What *did* scare me, though, was the feeling these revelations inspired in me. Or rather, the depth of that feeling—the extent to which I've fallen hard for this gorgeous, passionate, steel-willed stranger. This man I know I can never have for long. I push the thought of our impending separation far out of mind. I won't let it ruin the moment at hand.

"That's good," Cash murmurs, taking my face in his hands. "I never want you to be afraid of me, Maddie. You never have to be afraid of me. I know how to control myself. I've had to learn. And goddamn, has that control been tested.

"I know, Cash," I whisper, wrapping my fingers around his wrists.

And it's the truth, too. There may be nothing but raw power coursing beneath his sculpted exterior, but I know without needing proof that he would never turn it against me—or anyone else who didn't deserve it. Didn't he hold himself back from fighting Luke just yesterday? Didn't he rise above those asshole bikers the night we first met? His Dad may have passed down the reckless impulse to do harm, but Cash has trained himself to be better. This is a man who turned down a profitable business when it was offered on a silver platter, simply because it was the right thing to do, by his code. And that is a man I trust, implicitly.

I rest my cheek on Cash's shoulder as he pulls me into a swift embrace. He kisses the top of my head, a gesture that somehow feels more intimate than anything we've yet to share. I feel my body meld to his; fluid, eager, and so, *so* ready. My body has ceased to tremble, now. I've never felt more steady in my life.

Cash peels himself away from me just long enough to snap out the gray blanket, spreading it out across the sandy, pebble-studded shore. As he smooths out the well-worn fabric, I kick off my sandals and step up to him, running my hands down his broad back. He turns to me, eyes gleaming as I kneel on the blanket before him. Slipping out of his muddy shoes, he lowers himself to his knees as well, running his hands down along my sides. I plant my hands on the panes of his chest as he circles my waist with one arm, letting his other hand continue its journey down my body.

A low moan escapes my parted lips as Cash slides his hand beneath the band of my cotton shorts. I press my forehead to his shoulder, my back arching as he slides his hand between my thighs, letting his fingertips brush against the thin material of my underwear—the only scrap of fabric separating us now. My breath catches as Cash pushes aside the scant panel, resting two masterful fingers against my throbbing sex.

"Christ," Cash groans, running his fingers all along the length of me, "You're so wet for me, Maddie…"

"What do you expect?" I breathe, letting my head roll to the side as Cash strokes my aching sex.

"I've been thinking about this all week," he growls, holding me steady as my body goes liquid under his expert touch, "Thinking how fucking sexy you are when you're turned on. How much I love making you come…"

I gasp, clutching onto Cash's shoulders as he lays those two fingers firmly against my tender clit. Every word I've ever known falls away as he traces long, slow circles over that aching nub. Warm, blissful pleasure radiates through my body at his every stroke, my muscles clenching ecstatically around the delicious sensation.

"Relax…" he murmurs authoritatively in my ear, rubbing that excitable button with swift, firm loops. "Just let go, Maddie. Let me make you feel good…"

"It does. You do," I breathe, my knees going weak as searing pleasure mounts in my core, ready to spill out through my entire body. "It feels so good, Cash. I *love* your hands on me…"

But my words give way to a throaty cry as his two strong fingers slide back, driving up inside of me as he works my clit with his thumb. His fingers collide with that luscious spot just behind my navel, flexing deliciously as unrelenting pulses of sensation ring out through my body. I can feel myself speeding toward the edge of orgasm, unable to keep myself from tumbling over the cliff.

"I'm so close…" I gasp, bucking my hips against Cash's expert touch.

"Let go," he urges, bearing down on my screaming clit as his fingers slide even deeper inside of me, "Come for me, Maddie. I want to feel you…"

At his command, I let down my defenses, give into the rush of sensation that bursts through me. My every cell is infused with that rolling wave of bliss as it courses through me, carries me away on a sea of ecstatic pleasure. Cash lowers me onto my back as I'm overtaken by this feeling, pinning my hands above my head and kissing along my neck. I can feel his cock raging with desire against my trembling thigh as the orgasm passes through me, leaving my chest heaving and mouth spread with in a rapturous grin.

"You and your promises…" I manage to gasp.

"What did I tell you?" he grins, kissing the valley just below my collarbone.

"Just keep your hands on me," I plead, grinding my hips against his.

"Oh, I intend to," he murmurs, loosing my wrists and pushing my tiny tank top up over my breasts.

I pull the flimsy garment over my shoulders, casting it aside as Cash palms my modest but firm breasts. He lowers his lips to them, taking one nipple between his full lips as he lightly pinches the other. The warring sensations make my head spin—in the best way possible. I grab the edge of his t-shirt and pull it up over his head. The tee falls away, revealing Cash's gorgeously cut torso in all its inked, rippling glory. But that's not all I want to see of him.

With sure hands, I grab hold of his belt buckle and whip it open, loosing the button and zipper as fast as I can. Cash kneels before me as I tug the briefs and jeans down over his firm ass, my eyes transfixed by the staggering, pulsating cock standing at attention before me. I've never found a man's *manhood* to be beautiful before…but of course, Cash's is the exception. I run my hands along the smooth, rigid length, tracing the flushed bell head with my thumb. Cash groans as I work my hands along his shaft, his back arching with pleasure. I want to feel even more of him. All of him.

"Goddammit, Maddie…" he moans, as I lower my mouth to his cock, rubbing along the length of him all the while.

I let my blue eyes flick up to meet his as I part my lips and, ever-so-deliberately, take the swollen tip of him into my mouth. A shudder of bliss runs down my spine as I run my tongue along the ridge of his head. Low on my knees, I grab hold of his firm ass and pull as much of him into my mouth as I can. I can feel him pulsing against my tongue, taste his desire as it mounts. He buries his hands in my hair, tugging just hard enough for me to feel it.

"You've got me right on the edge," he rasps, as I run my tongue from the base of his shaft to the very tip of him.

"Maybe it's time you let go, too," I grin up at him, working my hands firmly down his throbbing cock, slick where my mouth has traversed it.

I cry out in delighted surprise as Cash grabs me by the hips and flips me onto my hands and knees. My back arches as he runs his fingers along my spine, letting me feel his slick cock pressing right up against my slit. I glance back at him over my shoulder, marveling at the sheer enormity of his form. At this moment, at the height of desire, he seems larger than life. An ancient god visiting the mortal world for the briefest of moments. But his godliness doesn't make me feel small or base. It elevates me. No—we raise *each other* up. And now, I want to see just how high we can soar.

"You want to feel me from behind?" he murmurs, running his hands over the rise of my ass. I catch my breath as he trails his fingers between my cheeks, letting the pad of his thumb brush against that tight circle of muscle no man has ever touched. Surprise gives way to deep satisfaction, a kind I've never known. How can being touched there feel so *good*?

"Y-you mean…?" I stammer, my pulse quickening. That's another thing I've never, ever tried. Not that I'm opposed, in theory…but—

"No, no," he murmurs, trailing kisses down my back, "We're not exactly equipped for that. Today, that is. I just want to take you, just like this. Watch my cock slide into you. Watch you writhe under me… Sound good?"

My imagination spins out of control, imagining all the new things Cash is going to teach me…Someday. But for now—

"God yes," I gasp, feeling my thighs begin to quake.

I hear the soft rip of a wrapper, and watch over my shoulder as Cash rolls a condom down his massive cock. That must be an XXL rubber, to accommodate such an impressive piece. But my speculations stop in their tracks as I feel the tip of that gigantic member pressed firmly against my wet, eager sex. I grab hold of the gray blanket, bunching handfuls of the fabric in my shaking fingers as Cash sets his hands firmly on my hips. For a moment suspended in time, I raise my eyes and look out across the lake. The sun is hovering just below the horizon, sending tendrils of orange and pink out across the sky. It's beautiful. Perfect. And that's even before—

Our voices rise up together, toward the canopy of leaves overhead, as Cash's cock parts my silky flesh. He presses into me with powerful, measured force, and my mouth falls open in an amazed "o" as I feel the unthinkable size of him. From behind, he feels even bigger, drives even deeper, but I don't shrink away in response. Instead, I press back against him, sending his cock even further into my ready body. He works himself inside of me inch by inch, until finally I feel the full length of him drive up into my very core. His fingers tighten around my hips as he sinks all the way in, filling me up completely.

"You're so goddamn tight," he groans.

"No—you're just hung as *fuck*," I laugh breathlessly, bucking against his powerful rod. "I'm surprised I can even fit you."

He meets my pass as I press firmly back against him, and we cry out in unison again. Our voices are low, guttural—absolutely primal. I've never heard these sounds coming out of my mouth before, but I don't feel self-conscious. I feel more like myself than ever before. Now that I've felt the full massiveness of Cash, I'm hooked. Faster and faster we thrust together, our bodies moving with harmonious, fervid purpose. My head falls back between my shoulders as I bounce on Cash's rigid cock, savoring the feel of him colliding with the very core of me. I swear, it feels like he could tear me right in two if we weren't careful.

"I'm right there, babe. I'm *right there*," Cash growls through gritted teeth.

"Come," I tell him in a hoarse whisper, "I want you to—"

The sky splits open before me as the sun crests over the horizon. My eyes open wide as Cash pounds into me with one last leveling thrust, driving so deeply that the newly broken day itself seems to spin wildly all around us. I feel him come hard as I push back against him with all my might, my muscles tightening around him. For a moment that feels like an hour, we float there together—balancing between one second, one day, and the next. Time itself steps aside for us, before rushing back in and leveling us completely.

Spent, Cash lowers himself to me, closing the space between our bodies. His hard chest presses against my back as our bodies rise and fall with fervent breath. Rolling onto his side, Cash pulls me against him, enclosing me with his arms as we look out over the crystalline lake together. Our breathing slows as the sun begins its ascent into the sky, rolling white clouds reflected in the still water.

"So here's an idea," I murmur, burrowing against Cash's sturdy form, "Let's just stay right here. Forever. OK?"

"Sounds like a plan to me," he laughs huskily, pulling himself onto one elbow and resting a hand on my hip.

"We can build a little lean-to, and forsake our entire lives, and just screw on the beach for eternity," I go on, pulling myself to sitting. "I'm game if you are."

"I can't even tell if you're kidding," Cash muses, running his hand along my naked thigh.

"Me either," I smile back at him. And though obviously I don't *literally* have forever in mind, I can't help wondering in this moment how long Cash and I actually have together. The first week of our vacation is drawing to a close, and it already feels like time is moving far too quickly. I've resisted thinking about what happens when this trip is over, because I can't bear the thought of only having one more week with this man.

"Christ, you're beautiful," he murmurs, his eyes fixed on my nude form, backlit by the breaking day.

A lot of guys tell me I'm cute, or even pretty... but beautiful? Really beautiful? Not so much. How many times does anyone get to hear that in her life and feel it's sincere?

"What's the saying? 'Take a picture, it'll last longer'?" I laugh giddily, a little bashful at his praise.

"Got a camera?" Cash asks, a devilish grin spreading across his face.

I feel myself blushing at what he's proposing. I'm no prude about nude pics in theory. I've just never personally been one for trading naked pictures, not even with my long-term boyfriends. It always just seemed like a recipe for disaster—especially with the nature of the internet these days. I never trusted any of my exes enough to share such intimate material. What if one of them was a secret revenge-porn enthusiast? But Cash is a different story. Not only do I feel like—no, *know* I can trust him, but he also makes me want to live at full volume, try things I never have before.

"My phone's in my shorts pocket…" I grin back, cocking a mischievous eyebrow.

Cash stares at me, jaw wide open, looking like a man who's just won the lottery. "Are you fucking serious?" he asks, sitting upright. "You'd let me—?"

"Go ahead," I tell him, daringly.

In a flash, Cash grabs my cell and turns back to me. My own jaw swings dangerously close to the ground as he straightens up, not a stitch of clothing on him. His tall, perfectly balanced form is as gorgeous as I've ever seen it—which makes sense, as I'm getting to see more of it than ever before. Last time we were naked together, we were a few drinks in and lit by a neon light on the fritz. But now, in the clear light of early day, he's almost too perfect to take in all at once.

"OK," Cash smiles, lowering himself back onto the blanket before me, "You ready?"

I unlock the phone for him and sit cross-legged on the blanket, unsure of what to do next. I'm not really well versed in the grammar of sexy pouts and poses.

"I guess you probably can tell this is another thing I don't have much experience with," I laugh nervously.

"Really?" he asks. "You never sent nude pics to any of your boyfriends?"

"Nope," I shrug. "Not that they didn't ask."

"No kidding," he laughs softly.

"Is there, like, some kind of protocol for this?" I kid in my best porn star voice, fluttering my eyelashes ridiculously. But Cash doesn't seem interested in any of that.

"I like that you don't know the protocol," he says, "You're don't have to play at being sexy. You just…are."

I let my joking fall away, truly touched by Cash's response. I've always been pretty confident with my own sexuality, but I haven't been completely immune to the idea of "being sexy". There's so much pressure on women to perform sexiness, rather than feel good in their own skin. Cash is the first person I've been with, who doesn't make me feel like I'm falling short of some predetermined mark by just being myself. I sit before him, calm and composed, as he trains the camera on me.

"Perfect," he murmurs, glancing up from the screen.

"Just like this?" I ask. My blonde hair is sex-tousled, my makeup next to non-existent.

"Just like that," he says softly, focusing the shot.

I train my eyes on the camera, hands resting on my knees. It's not a glamorous, practiced shot—but it is real. And is this moment, I absolutely believe that I'm as beautiful as Cash tells me I am. Now *that's* something that's never happened to me before.

He takes a few more shots, smiling down at the screen. "Got it," he says, scrolling back through the half dozen shots. "Now I've just got to pick the best…"

Cash trails off mid-sentence, brow furrowing as he peers down at the screen. His expression goes from confused, to disbelieving, to completely blank in the space of a second. At first, I have no idea what he's reacting to so strongly…until, that is, I remember the last picture I took on that phone.

"Oh shit…" I squeak, hands flying to my mouth. The morning after we first slept together, I snapped that picture of him for Allie. I never thought it would come back to bite me. But isn't that always the way?

"Care to explain this?" Cash asks, turning the phone to face me.

There on the screen is the picture I look of Cash's sleeping form the morning after our "one night stand". The one I sent to Allie as proof of my making good on our bet. Even in the moment, I knew it was a shady move. And that was when I thought I'd never see the guy again. But now…

"I am so, so sorry Cash," I sputter, scrambling onto my knees.

"You took a naked picture of me? Without my knowing?" he asks evenly, though of course he already knows the answer. He has the evidence right there in his hand.

"I know. It was stupid," I hurry on, grabbing for the phone and missing, "I wasn't thinking, at all. It was an impulsive, reckless—"

But Cash's roaring laughter cuts me off mid-babble. He throws back his head and crows to the heavens, clutching his perfect stomach at the hilariousness of my gaff.

"You little creep!" he cackles, lunging forward and scooping me up in his arms.

"You were just messing with me?!" I shriek, pounding playfully at his chest with my fists. "Goddammit, Cash!"

"Yeah, well, that's what you get for being a sneaky little perv," he teases, holding the phone just out of my reach as I try and make a grab for it. What with his being an entire foot taller than me, it's not much of a contest.

"I thought you were seriously mad at me for a second," I say, standing on my tip toes to reach my phone.

"Nah," he says, "I don't blame you for wanting to get this sexy bod of mine on record."

"You're such a dick," I laugh, jumping to my feet as Cash gives chase. We dart around the clearing in the all-together, belly-laughing all the while. The way Cash can go from serious to playful, solemn to soulful, is incredible. His ever-changing mood is the most enticing things about him, and the most challenging. But hey—challenges are my thing, right?

"Truce! Truce. You can keep the picture," he finally allows, coming to a stop. "Just as long as I get to send this one of you to myself…"

"Fine, fair is fair,—" I reply, holding up my hands. Cash taps a few keys and raises a victorious fist into the air.

"There it goes!" he crows, handing my phone over at last, "That sucker is all mine."

"Oh god," I groan, clutching my phone to my bare chest, "Now the NSA has seen me in my birthday suit."

"Lucky motherfuckers, if you don't mind my saying," Cash grins, giving me a playful pat on the ass before going to fetch his clothes.

"Ha, ha," I drawl, rolling my eyes, "Whatever, it's fine. Now you have something to remember me by, I guess."

"What're you, swimming back to Seattle from here?" he laughs, pulling on his jeans, "What do you mean remember you—"

"Since we won't be seeing each other after the trip, I mean," I blurt out unthinkingly. The blunt certainty of my statement comes off way harsher than I meant it to. Fiddling with my own clothes, I stammer on, "I meant to remember me by…after."

Cash's body tenses for a fraction of a second, but that's all it takes for the spell of our gorgeous morning to be shattered. I invoked our relationship's inevitable deadline, here of all places. Now I feel as though I've ruined everything.

"Right," Cash says gruffly, pulling his tee back over his head.

"I just meant, you know, that I'm not expecting anything here," I say, stepping into my clothes as quickly as possible.

"Yeah, I got it," he goes on, tucking his hands into his pockets as I finish dressing.

"Are you mad that I said—? I didn't mean to—"

"It's fine, Maddie," he tells me, his expression neutral, "I wasn't expecting you to ride off into the sunset with me either."

"No…I know," I reply, giving my hair a nervous tousle.

"You've got a whole life of your own back in Washington," he goes on, rolling up the blanket. I hop off quickly to avoid being rolled up with it. "And I've got my own shit back home, too. Nothing as impressive as your job, but still. I've got a good thing going."

"No one's saying you don't," I reply, crossing my arms tightly.

"Course not," he smiles placidly, tucking the blanket back under his arm.

We're squared off across the clearing, our closeness of a moment ago scattered to the morning breeze. There's so much that we're not saying, so much of ourselves that we're still trying to protect. At least, that's what I'm doing. Cash has retreated back behind his unreadable mask, so I can't even guess at what he's thinking.

"We should head back," he says shortly, turning toward the canoe, "Before everyone else wakes up."

"Right," I say, following in his stride.

Everyone else: the real reason why we could never be together past this wonderful couple weeks.

Chapter Nine

Though mentioning the inevitable conclusion of our fling *right* after having incredible sex was a bit of a fumble, my misstep isn't without its up side. Knowing that we only have a little more than a week in each other's company adds a major exponent onto mine and Cash's want of each other. All of a sudden, we're locked in a race to see just how much mind-blowing sex we can have before distance and circumstance separate us.

And it seems that the answer is: quite a bit.

My secret excursions with Cash become a regular occurrence. I don't think I sleep for the next few days, I'm too excited to hear his telltale knock on my bedroom door. At first, we contain our liaisons to the dead of night, when we know everyone else in the house will be sleeping. But soon enough, it becomes clear that a few hours of the day just won't cut it. Cash's early efforts at throwing the others off our trail peter out as our days together tick away. We're still careful around our family members, feigning indifference to each other during group meals and activities. But the second we find ourselves alone again, it's a whole other story.

We steal away whenever we can, our hunger for each other only increasing each time it's sated. No place is safe from the urgency of our need. We have each other in the bed of the family's pickup truck, in remote corners of the woods accessed by ATV, even in the outdoor shower stall on one rather reckless occasion. We both know that it's risky, that one of our parents or siblings could very well catch on (or catch us in the act), but the awkwardness of that outcome doesn't come close to outweighing even a second Cash and I get to spend together. Besides, we're doing our due diligence not to get caught. Getting caught would mean being forced apart—and that's not an option. Not now. Not yet.

As the first half of my two-week vacation draws nearer, I find that I've completely acclimated to this strange domestic arrangement. Whereas the idea of John Hawthorne and my mom having a little summer fling totally freaked me out at the beginning of the week, given my feelings for Cash, I can hardly muster up the energy to care by now. Life out here by the lake plays out with its own set of rules. It's easy enough to imagine that the eight of us are the only people on the planet.

We're so isolated out here that I feel my anxieties about any taboos Cash and I are toying with falling by the wayside. So what if my mom and John were high school sweethearts? So what if they've been all moony-eyed during our week here? I know my mother well enough to be certain that it isn't really serious. The only thing in her life that she tended with any consistency at all was her relationship with my father. There's no chance in hell that she could replicate that with any other man. Especially not John Hawthorne.

On the second Saturday night of my stay at the Hawthorne lake house, I find myself with a couple hours to kill before my next rendezvous with Cash. He and his brothers are helping John with a small contracting job in town that needed a few extra hands. Even a few hours of separation from Cash is making me crawl up the walls. I try to distract myself by diving into *Love in the Time of Cholera*, one of my favorite Gabriel García Márquez novels. But even the absorbing, magic realism of his prose isn't enough to tear my thoughts away from Cash.

But wouldn't you know it, a different sort of distraction offers itself up to me (whether I like it or not). For the first time this week, it's just us Porter ladies hanging around the house, without the company of the Hawthorne men. And my mother pounces on the opportunity for a little "girl talk".

"Maddie!" I hear her call up the stairs as I root through my suitcase for some sexy underthings, "Come on down to the front porch, honey!"

"In a minute," I call back, holding up a bright red thong for consideration. A bit too on-the-nose, I decide. Cash and I are planning on visiting some local dive bar later, a place he frequents whenever he's back in his hometown. This is the first time we'll be in public as a pair since that first night at the roadside bar. I don't know why, but I'm super turned on by the idea of being seen together in the "real world". It'll make it feel like this isn't all just some crazy dream I've wandered into. But seeing as I'm already excited to spend some more alone time with Cash, I want to be prepared for what might come after. Pun *absolutely* intended.

I hear the warm sound of female conversation as I make my way down the stairs and step out onto the front porch. Four wooden Adirondack chairs are arranged along the verandah and occupied by my mom and sisters. Set on a low wicker table between them is quite a feast—fruit, cheese, chocolate, and four bottles of wine. I raise an eyebrow at Mom, watching as Anna and Sophie pour themselves generous glasses.

"What?" she says, waving off my skeptical look, "Can't we indulge a little for once? How often do I get to have all my girls in the same place? Come on. Let me spoil you a little."

"I'm not complaining," Sophie laughs, piling a plate with fresh strawberries and real whipped cream.

"Just don't narc on little nineteen-year-old me," Anna smiles, "This being my first taste of alcohol ever, obviously."

"I'm sure," Mom replies, rolling her eyes.

I wave my suspicion aside, never one to complain about free booze and snacks. I sink down into the last available chair as my family's conversation resumes.

"I think it's very smart of you, getting some extra credits over the summer," Mom says to Sophie, propping her feet up on the porch railing.

"I just want the option of graduating early, if anything good comes up," Sophie replies, sipping her wine, "Acting apprenticeships are pretty competitive. If I snag a good one in the middle of senior year, I want to be able to grab it."

"Campus must be pretty quiet in the summer," Mom goes on, "I'm sure it'll be relaxing to get some alone time."

"Not that you'll be *entirely* without company," Anna remarks, her voice purposefully casual. I catch Sophie shooting her an evil glare.

"Oh! Will some of your friends be doing the summer session too?" Mom asks cheerfully. "How fun."

"Uh. Kind of," Sophie says vaguely, looking as though she wants to dive head first into her glass of wine. "It, uh, turns out that Luke is going to be TA-ing some more classes this session…And he's going to be an RA, too."

"RA? What's that?" Mom asks.

"A resident assistant," Sophie says, her voice pained, "It means he'll be living in the dorms, too. Making sure us kiddos don't get into any trouble."

I have to try hard not to giggle at Sophie's discomfort. I've barely seen her look at Luke all week. I'm sure having him around her on campus all summer isn't exactly a dream come true. Though from the way Luke's been looking at *her*, I doubt he minds too much. I've been so wrapped up in my fling with Cash that I've dropped the ball on getting to the bottom of their drama. I make a mental note to get the truth out of Sophie before the week is up.

"Get out," Mom breathes, grabbing Sophie's hand, "That is so, so wonderful. And here I thought all you kids were going to go your separate ways after this week. I'm so glad you two will get to keep on being friends."

"Uh-huh," my middle sister says, a hot blush rising in her cheeks.

"I guess Sophie and Luke will have to be the ones keeping in touch for all of us, huh?" Anna goes on, her tone unreadable, "Since the rest of us will be going home after this?"

"Seems that way," I add, trying to keep my voice as neutral as hers.

A small smile lifts the corner of Mom's mouth. "Well, actually…" she says conspiratorially, "I wanted to talk to you girls about just that."

My sisters and I trade uneasy glances. Mom has that brand-new-scheme glint in her eye. And that's never a good thing for the rest of us. I survey the bounty of booze and treats with a fresh wave of wariness. Has she just been trying to butter us up with this "girls night"? And if so, what is she about to spring on us now?

"What's up, Mom?" Sophie asks uneasily.

"Well," Mom begins, taking a big swig of her wine, "I know I told you that my plan for this summer was to spend a little time getting grounded in my hometown before going back to Vermont. Really, I just wanted a couple of weeks away from it all. At first."

"Are you staying for longer, then?" Anna asks, "Did you find another place to rent in town or something?"

"Or something," Mom beams at us. "Actually…God, I feel like a teenager again, dishing with you girls like this. But actually, things have been going so well for me and John here that he's…he's invited me to stay!"

My sisters and I stare blankly at our mother, unmoving.

"You mean like, for another couple of weeks…?" I ask, my voice hollow.

"And another, and another," Mom grins happily, sinking back in her chair.

"Mom, just cut to the chase, OK?" Sophie says heatedly, "Exactly how long are you going to stay here playing house with John?"

"Watch your tone," Mom scolds her, taken aback by her reaction, "But since you ask, I'm planning on staying indefinitely."

That word, *indefinitely*, echoes across the wide front lawn as my sisters and I try to comprehend it.

"But…You don't live here," Anna says, eyes wide, "You live in Vermont. In our house. The house we've always lived in."

"Yes, dear," Mom says, her voice hardening, "I *know*. I have been living in that house much longer than any of you. And since you're planning to move out to go 'find yourself', Anna, I'd soon be living there all alone. Or I would have been, if John hadn't offered—"

"Are you… Selling our house?" I ask softly, knowing that I sound for the world like a wounded child.

"I am planning to sell the house, yes," Mom says coolly.

"But that's—you can't—were you even going to talk to us about it?!" Sophie cries.

"That's what I'm doing now," Mom explains. "Not that I need your permission, but I'm taking my time weighing the decision to—"

"Really? Because it seems to me like you've already made your choice," Sophie shoots back, "We love that house, Mom. Our whole childhoods, our entire lives with Dad were there. That place is all we have left of him. We can't lose—"

"Don't tell *me* about loss," Mom snaps suddenly, her voice high and shrill. I feel my body go utterly still. I know this change that comes over her too well. One minute it's sunshine and happiness, the next it's resentment and rage. She goes on, uninterested in pulling any punches now. "I know all about *loss*, thank you. Your father was the love of my life, from the time I was just a girl. You'll never be able to feel the loss of him the way I have."

"Christ, Mom…" I breathe, staring at her aghast, "Are you seriously making our grief into a pissing contest right now?"

"Of course not," she snaps, swigging her wine, "Because it's no contest whatsoever. Your father is a part of your past. You can all move on and lead long, happy lives now. But he was my future. My entire future. I've lost more than you can possibly imagine, losing him."

Her words hit me like a punch to the gut, and I have to steady myself against the armrest to keep from falling over—or else throwing myself at her. Sophie and Anna are rooted in their seats, looking appalled, disappointed, but most of all hurt. That does it for me. No one gets to hurt my little sisters, even if that someone happens to be our mother. I draw myself up and fix my eyes on her, finally putting voice to the words I've wanted to throw at her for so long.

"What would you even know about what we've all been going through since Dad died?" I ask her, the evenness of my voice surprising even me. "In the past three years, you haven't bothered to check in with any of us about how we were doing. Not once. You don't know the first thing about how his death has changed our lives."

"Please," Mom scoffs, "I think I know my own daughters—"

"Did you know I've been seriously depressed for the last three years?" I cut her off, my hands balling into fists, "Did you know that I barely made it through the first semester back at school after he died? That I almost dropped out just before graduating? I talked about being a literature professor like him, for my entire life. Did you ever wonder why I suddenly changed my mind and punted to marketing? It's because reading the books he loved, following in his footsteps, was too painful for me once he was gone. His death has changed my entire life. My entire future. Not a day goes by that I don't think of him. And all that's to say nothing of your other two daughters."

Mom's mouth straightens into a hard line as she glances at Sophie and Anna. "Is this how you girls feel as well?" she asks crisply, "That I've been 'negligent to your needs' since Archie passed away? Hmm?"

"I don't know if you can say 'negligent'…" Anna replies, fixing Mom with a cool stare, "Since you never considered our needs in the first place. I'd say indifferent, if anything."

"That's ridiculous!" Mom cries.

"Why bother asking if you're just going to shoot us down?" Anna snaps back. "The truth is, Mom, that *we've* been taking care of *you* since Dad died."

"Especially Anna," Sophie jumps in, "I got to run off to drama school and deal with shit on my own, but she was left to pick up the pieces while you collapsed. We know that Dad's passing was hard on you. Of course it was. But how can you say that we didn't feel it too? How can you know so little about your own kids and not even care?"

"Well," Mom says, setting her wine glass down on the porch and standing to go, "If this is the way you feel, then I'd think you'd be happy to be rid of me. I'll stay here with John, and take myself off your hands for good."

"For good? Mom, be serious," Sophie cries, exasperated, "You've had plenty of flings since dad died. How is this one any different? You're putting our family, our home, everything at stake for him. Please, just take a second to consider—"

"You've given me plenty to consider tonight," Mom cuts her off. "I've apparently failed you as a mother, isn't that right? You'd be better off without me?"

"That's not what we're saying at all, Mom," I tell her, a hard knot finally beginning to form in my throat, "What I've wanted more than anything else since dad died was my mother. I've always wanted you to be a part of my life. Please don't make that impossible."

"I see," Mom replies, looking around at all of us disdainfully, "Well, girls. Thank you for making this decision so easy for me. Since I'm apparently incapable of being a good mother to you, I'll just go ahead and bow out. Seeing as I'm *impossible*. Anna, you're more than welcome to stay at the Vermont house until it's sold. Though I suggest finding other accommodations quickly. I'm sure that property will get snatched up quick."

And just like that, she turns on her heel and marches away from us. Turning her back just like she's done a thousand times before. I can feel my heart straining at the fault lines where it's already been broken—by Dad's death, the dissolution of our family, the distance that's built up between me and my beloved sisters. Even though our mother's alive and well, I feel like I'm about to lose her now, too. Although judging by the ease with which she walks away from us now, maybe that already happened a long time ago.

"I just… I can't believe her," Sophie says, silent tears streaming down her cheeks.

"I can," Anna replies flatly, taking a big sip of wine, "As far as I'm concerned, this is pretty in-character for good ol' Robin."

"Do you think she'll really stay here with John?" I ask them, heart rattling in my chest. "Maybe she's just bluffing."

"Now she'll stay, just to spite us," Sophie scoffs through her tears. "Where do you think you got your competitive streak from, Maddie? We've dared to challenge her. Now we're the ones who are going to pay."

I lean heavily against the chair, feeling panic growing in the pit of my stomach. Against my own good sense, I'd let some little part of myself start to believe that this trip didn't need to be the end of me and Cash. If our parents were simply going to part ways after this, maybe there could have been some future for us. Stranger things have happened, right? But so long as Mom and John's relationship is moving forward, harboring fantasies about a future with Cash is just asking for heartbreak down the line.

And if this well-worn heart of mine breaks one more time, I'm not sure there will be any putting it back together again.

"Fuck her," Sophie spits suddenly, "If she cares that little about us, why don't we just follow her lead?

What if we just took a stand and cut her out of our lives, right now? If the three of us broke off from her, think of how much happier—"

"If any of us could stand to abandon her completely, we would have already," I cut Sophie off, "No matter how badly she hurts us, she's still family. That's not something you can ever forget."

A long silence engulfs us. I can see in my sisters' pained eyes that they know this truth as well as I do— family isn't something you get to choose for yourself. Even if you estrange yourself, disown your roots, run as far away as you can, you can never entirely sever that bond. Didn't the three of us come running to this lake house the minute our mother called? Didn't the Hawthorne boys flock back here too, despite their toxic relationships with John? Like it or not, we are all our parents children.

The question now is, how do we learn to live with that?

The growl of the Hawthornes' pickup truck sounds out in the night, rumbling up the driveway toward us. Through the mud-specked windshield, I can see that Cash is riding shotgun while John drives. Luke and Finn are riding in the truck bed with some leftover construction materials. One look at John's solemn, weathered face is all it takes to send Anna dashing off into the house. She can't even bear the sight of the man who's helping our mother disassemble our past. Sophie goes stock still as the pickup pulls to a stop in the driveway. But the second the Hawthorne men start walking our way, she bolts as well.

I'm the sole sentry guarding John's path as he approaches, flanked by his sons. My arms are crossed tightly across my chest, barely reigning in my clamoring heart. I take in the sight of this upstanding, bearded woodsman, conflicting emotions churning through my blood. On the one hand, I'm grateful that my mother's found someone she cares about, assuming that she does. I never expected or wanted her to be alone for the rest of her life. Truly, I'd be thrilled if she found a good man to love.

But at the same time, I'm having trouble believing that John is that man. After everything Cash has told me about his father—the abuse, the distrust, the coldness—I can't imagine how he could be good for my sensitive, flighty mother. I mean, John *must* know that selling the Vermont house would crush me and my sisters. The only thing he's truly ignorant to is what *else* a union between him and my mother would ruin. Namely, any chance of Cash being part of my life, in the way I want him to be.

"Hey there, Maddie," John says from the bottom step, turning his handsome, rugged face toward me, "You holding down the fort for us?"

"Something like that," I reply, hugging my arms even tighter to my chest. I watch Cash's brow furrow as he picks up on my distress. I can't hide a damn thing from him. Not ever.

"Where's Robin and the girls?" John goes on, noticing the array of untouched food and wine on the porch, "I thought you were going to have yourselves a girls night or something?"

"Girls night was kind of a bust," I tell them.

"Oh. What happened?" Luke asks, tucking his hands into his pockets. He tries to sound unattached, but I'm sure his mind is on Sophie. He's protective of her, for whatever reason. And while I may not know the specifics of their relationship, I can't say I'm not glad that there's *someone* looking out for her.

"Well," I say shortly, "Mom broke the news about moving in here with your dad. Permanently. *And* selling our childhood home. So that kind of put a damper on things."

All three boys' whip around to face their father, whose face hardens into stone.

"Dad…What?" Luke asks his father.

"Ah, shit…" John sighs, rubbing his jaw, "I meant to tell you boys myself, but—"

Without saying a word, Finn walks off around the house, his face unreadable. Luke stares at his father, rightfully indignant. But Cash's eyes swing back to my face instead. He knows as well as I do that our parents getting more serious means an end to us. For good. And the angry sorrow roiling in his eyes is enough to do me in. I try and blink back the tears that gather in my eyes, but I know the levees won't hold for long.

"Dad, I really don't know about this," Luke says, trying to remain diplomatic.

"There's nothing for you to know about," John shoots back gruffly, "Robin and I decided, and now it's done."

"OK, but… It's our home too," Luke says slowly, his hands clenching.

"Is it?" John laughs in his middle son's face, "I didn't realize. Do you build this damn place up out of nothing? Have you ever paid a cent to live here?"

"All I mean is, this place is important to all of us," Luke goes on heatedly. "You could have done us the courtesy of asking—"

"*Asking*?" John growls, rounding on Luke. "You want me to ask you for your *blessing* to do as I please in my own goddamn house?"

A jolt of real fear pierces me as John loses control of his temper. Cash has told me stories about his dad's anger issues, the way he can be totally calm one minute and throwing punches the next. So far, I've never seen it happen…but I get the feeling that's about to change.

"Of course not, Dad," Luke tells his father, "But—"

"But nothing," John shouts, taking a looming step toward his son. Though the Hawthorne boys each clear six feet easily, John is still the tallest by a couple of inches. His shoulders are squared as he all but snarls down at his middle son, "You may pull your weight around here, Luke, but don't get to thinking that I need your say-so to do anything I goddamn please."

"Don't get in my face, Dad," Luke warns his father, holding his ground.

"What's that?" John snarls, giving Luke a hard shove in the chest.

"Hey!" Cash snaps, taking a quick step toward them.

"Stay out of this," John tells his oldest son.

Luke lifts his chin defiantly, unwilling to back down. I grab hold of the porch railing, adrenaline coursing through my body. I've never been around this sort of raw, physical aggression before. And I certainly don't want to be now.

"You think I owe you some kind of explanation?" John goes on, backing Luke across the lawn, "I've put a roof over your heads and food on your plates for twenty-six goddamn years. I'm handing over my business—the business I built from scratch—right on over to you without you having to lift a finger. Don't tell me I owe you *anything*."

"Without having to lift a *finger*?" Luke snaps, stopping dead in his tracks, "I've been busting my ass for that business since I was a kid. I've devoted my whole life to this family. Do you have any idea—"

"Don't you raise your goddamn voice to me," John snarls, jabbing a finger into Luke's hard chest.

"Don't *you* lay a fucking finger on me," Luke shoots back, knocking his father's arm away. "Haven't you had your fill of beating up on—"

I leap back as John throws himself at Luke, tackling him to the ground. They roll across the grass, a tangle of limbs and flying fists. Cash lunges toward them at top speed, throwing himself into the fray.

"*Get the fuck off him, Dad!*" he roars, dragging his father away from Luke.

John loses his footing as Cash gets hold of him. Luke scrambles to his feet as his dad rounds on Cash, swinging wildly. Cash dodges every blow—and I can see now that he's used to countering his father's attacks. John moves through these motions without remorse, without surprise. It's something the Hawthorne boys have been trained to expect all their lives. But as many times as John swings at Cash, Cash refuses to stoop to his level. He finally manages to pin his father's arms behind his back, though the restraining hold only seems to make John angrier.

"*Let me go,*" he roars, writhing furiously.

"Not until you stand down," Cash answers, his voice surprisingly calm. I realize that it wasn't just his childhood that prepared him to take on his dad, it was his Army training too. Cash could probably level John with what he learned in the military, but he refuses to pick on a weaker man…whether weaker of body or weaker of character.

"Now you want to be fucking noble," John growls, pulling free of Cash at last and pacing away from his sons, "After throwing away everything I gave you, wasting every opportunity, and fucking up the one thing you ever did commit to, you want to come back here and save the day? Not gonna happen, kid."

"Don't worry Dad," Cash says through gritted teeth, "I gave up on trying to save you a long time ago."

Wordless rage smothers John's response. The weathered old man spits on the grass at his feet and turns away, storming off into the house. I cringe away as he brushes past me, my whole being repulsed by him. He doesn't know the first thing about his oldest son. How noble he really is. And to think, he and my mother are the reason we'll never be together the way we want.

Maybe they really *do* deserve each other.

"Thanks," Luke says gruffly, rubbing his shoulder, "For the assist, I mean."

"Of course," Cash says, matter-of-factly, "You may be a big dumb jock, but you're still my brother."

Luke lets out a short laugh and, to my surprise, throws his arms around Cash. They hug quickly, fiercely—pounding each other on the back before breaking away. Luke doesn't even look at me as he takes off around the house. I have the feeling his mind is otherwise occupied. As he rounds the corner and disappears from sight, the fear and anxiety that I've been holding back come flooding through my body. I sink down onto the porch steps, letting my face fall into my hands. Tears stream through my fingers, unable to be contained, as Cash rushes to me.

"It's all right," he murmurs, wrapping me up in his arms, "It's all right, Maddie."

"H-how can you say that?" I sob, curling against the shelter of his body, "Everything's going to shit, Cash."

"Last time I checked," he replies, smoothing the hair out of my face, "Everything's shit more often than not. Guess I'm just used to it."

"But *why*," I insist, pulling back to look up at his gleaming hazel eyes, "Why get used to it? Why settle for being miserable your whole life?"

"I didn't realize I was living such a miserable life," he says, jaw pulsing.

"Your dad just tried to beat the shit out of you and Luke," I cry, "He's invited a woman you barely know to live in your home—"

"This isn't my home, Maddie," Cash tells me firmly, "And that man I just kept from punching Luke's teeth in? He may be my father, but I gave up on him acting like a decent dad a long time ago."

"So you just don't care?" I press him, pulling away from his tight embrace, "Our parents are ruining any chance of us being in each others' lives once this trip is over, and that's just fine by you?"

"Last I heard from you, that was out of the question anyway," he shoots back angrily, sitting back away from me. "You made it pretty clear that you didn't want to see me again once we leave here, Maddie."

"I thought that's what *you* wanted," I tell him, "Shit, Cash. This thing between us was supposed to be a one night stand. No strings attached. How was I supposed to tell you that I was starting to fall for you?"

His gaze is hard on my face as I realize what I've said. What I've owned up to.

"You should have just told me," he says firmly, "That's what you should have done. Instead of trying to guess at what I wanted, or just assuming that I wanted a quick, easy fuck 'cause I'm a guy. That's where you fucked up, Maddie."

"I-I'm sorry," I tell him, blinking back the next wave of tears.

"I've always been honest with you," he shoots back, his face stony, "I've been more honest with you than anyone. Ever. Why don't you trust me enough to do the same?"

"I didn't know I'd be able to trust you, Cash," I say around the knot in my throat, "You were just a handsome stranger at a bar. I didn't think you'd turn out to be...*you*."

"And now?" he demands, planting his elbows on his knees, "Do you trust me now?"

"Of course," I breathe, placing my hands on his arm. But he tugs away from me; my fingers close around air.

"Then why don't you tell me what it is you actually want here, Maddie?" he says, his tone cool and measured, "No games, for once. Give me the truth. Do you want to cut this thing off when we leave here or not?"

"Even if we both wanted to see this through," I begin shakily, "It's out of our hands, now. Our parents will be living together, Cash. As a couple. Don't you know what that means? We can't keep seeing each other, let alone—"

"That's not what I asked, dammit," he growls, shoving a hand through his dark curls, "I asked what *you* wanted, Maddie."

"How can I know that?" I cry, exasperated, "The thing I would *really* want isn't even possible any—"

"Just say it," he presses, hands clenched angrily, "What do you *want*."

"I want you to have been a stranger," I say in a rush, reaching for his hardened fists, "I want you to be anything but a Hawthorne. I want to be anything but a Porter. But there's nothing we can do to change that, Cash. Nothing."

"It's not as cut and dry as that," he says, grabbing hold of my hands, "We don't have to give them that power over us. You can't choose your family, Maddie. But you can choose to leave it behind."

"What?" I breathe, "What do you mean, leave it behind?"

"Just what I said," he goes on fiercely, "We don't owe them anything, Maddie. Our parents. We've had to fend for ourselves all this time, keep afloat however we could. They've only ever weighed us down. Why not cast them off?"

"You really think you could do that?" I challenge him, "Cut your father out of your life, just like that?"

"He cut himself out," Cash says firmly, "I don't mind returning the favor."

"And your brothers?" I demand, "You could turn your back on them, too? Luke and Finn, the men you've been protecting your whole life?"

"I don't—I wouldn't—" Cash stammers, his voice faltering for the first time since I've known him. "They're not a part of this."

"We all are," I tell him, my voice heavy with remorse, "You can't just carve out part of your family, without hurting the lot of them. You know that, Cash."

"I don't know any such goddamn thing," he snaps back, "But at least *I'm* willing to figure it out. I'm willing to try for *you*, Maddie."

"You say that…" I say softly, "But I can't shake the feeling that I know how this will end, Cash. If we try to keep going. It's going to end in us getting hurt. *Bad*."

"So you'd just as soon give up," he says. It's a statement, not a question. And a statement I have absolutely no response to.

"Cash," I plead, "Please, try and understand. This thing between us…it's huge. The kind of huge that could make or break a lifetime. And right now, we're toeing the point of no return. If we take one more step, we could ruin each other…"

"Or?" he says, his voice low and rasping.

"It's too hard to think about 'or'," I whisper, "Because I know that 'or' could be the best thing that ever happened to me…but I'll never get to know for sure."

"So I don't get a say in this," he snarls, tearing his eyes away from my face, "You're just going to do whatever the hell you want, is that it? Whatever keeps you from feeling an ounce of pain? Jesus, Maddie. Getting anything at all worth *having* is gonna hurt like a bitch. I know you're strong enough to take it. Why can't you just trust yourself to be—"

"I don't know," I cry out, leaping to my feet, "All I know is…That I need a second, here. I need to think. I need…I need to get out of this place."

"You want to leave? Just like that?" Cash asks, taken aback, "Maddie—"

"I can't stay," I tell him, pacing the dew-soaked grass, "What just happened with me and my mom, everything she said…And your dad, Christ—I don't even know if I feel safe around him. I can't think about something as important and you and me with all this shit going on—"

"If you leave now," Cash says, catching me by the arms, "How do I know I'll ever see you again?"

"You don't," I whisper, keeping my eyes trained on his, "I can't give you any certainty, Cash. I can't leave you with anything but your own faith in us. I'm…I'm so sorry."

He stares at me for a long, hard moment, searching deep into my soul for an answer, an explanation…but there's none to be found. I have no idea what's going to happen next; to me, to him, to our families. But I'm certain that I have to go. Right now. I'm drowning, here. I can't clear my head until I'm back on dry land, back in my real life that I've built in Seattle. The life that doesn't include Cash Hawthorne.

His eyes harden as he realizes that there's nothing he can do. He lets his hands drop from my arms, takes a step away from me. The first step of many that will carry us both back to the lives we know. The ache in my core as this new, irresolvable distance springs up between us is wrenching, nearly intolerable. I can only hope that each step gets a little easier…whether they lead us back to each other or not.

"Fine," he rasps, rubbing his sharp jaw. "Do what you're going to do, Porter. Just don't expect me to show up begging at your doorstep. I'm not the type to get down on my knees."

And with that, he turns away from me. He strides across the wide lawn with cold purpose, ripping open the driver's side door of the pickup. The engine roars to life as blinding headlights tear through the gathering twilight. Without a parting glance, Cash peels out of the driveway, tearing off at top speed. As the sound of the racing truck fades away, nature's nighttime orchestra swells to fill the silence.

A hollow chasm tears open inside of me as I go to collect my things…I have a feeling that nothing will ever fill that space again.

Chapter Ten

No one even tries to stop me as I take my hasty leave from the lake house. My mom, John, the Hawthorne boys, and even my sisters have all scattered for the night. Everyone is busy licking their wounds behind closed doors. But hey—that's always how we've done things in the Porter house. Every woman for herself. Maybe we have more in common with the Hawthornes than I thought.

By rights, I should be a wreck right now; sobbing, screaming, and tearing out my hair. But as I haul my suitcase back to my car and settle in behind the wheel, I just feel…nothing. Nothing but an indifferent numbness. As I pull away from the Hawthorne house, I have the fleeting hope that Cash might intercept me on the way out. Maybe he'll have come up with some brilliant solution to our quandary. Maybe he'll block my way, refuse to let me go. Maybe he'll just hold me—nothing could seem hopeless with his arms around me.

But of course, Cash doesn't miraculously appear as I flee from the lake house, cutting our time here together in half. I set off to retrace my route home unimpeded. The man I've fallen for this week isn't a mirage, after all. He's not an ideal, unattainable fantasy. He's a person. A real, complicated, deeply flawed person who I desperately wish could be a part of my life.

Here's hoping I didn't just ruin the chances of making that wish come true.

I drive until my eyes are bleary with sleeplessness. As I hit the halfway point in my journey and cross the state line, a familiar neon sign catches my eye. "Drink Here," it commands from the side of the road. I let my lips open as a laugh rises in my throat—but the sound comes out as a ragged sob instead. As I speed past the bar where I first laid eyes on Cash, the place where we spent our first night together, my numbness finally gives way to sharp, slicing pain.

And here I thought I was going to get away with a little case of the blues.

I blow past the now-familiar motel, unwilling to take my foot off the gas. I couldn't bear to revisit the place where I first laid eyes on Cash. The room where we spent our first night together. It's stupid to keep driving in this state—reckless, even. But at this point, I'm racing my despair home. If I can just make it through the next eight hours, I can fall to pieces in the familiar mouse hole that is my lonely apartment. The comfort of privacy is all I can hope for now.

It's early Sunday morning before I ease open the front door of my Seattle studio once again. My body aches from my desperate flight as I wrangle my suitcase through the door. Everything is just as I left it a week ago, down to the empty bottle of wine on the counter. But the normalcy of this place doesn't stabilize me the way I thought it would. It's all the more disorienting, stepping back into the flow of my real life. Going from the whirlwind, breathtaking, full-throttle spree of this past week to the mind-numbingly normal is giving me serious emotional whiplash. For lack of a better idea, I leave my suitcase by the door and sprawl out on my narrow bed. I can't muster the will to do much else.

The second I hear my phone chirp, however, a bolt of energy lights me up from the inside. I spring across the room, praying that Cash has sent some word, any word at all. But my hope dashes itself on the rocks as I look down at the screen and see Sophie's name.

Sophie: Where are you?

Swallowing a sigh, I tap out a short reply.

Me: Home. I needed to leave early.

Sophie: Are you OK?

Me: Not really. Are you?

Sophie: Pretty far from it. I'm bailing early too. Heading back to school.

Me: And Anna?

Sophie: Heading back home on her own. Mom meant what she said about staying.

Me: Talk about going our separate ways.

Sophie: Yeah.

I can't think of what else to tell my little sister. I almost wish I could confide in her about what's been going on with Cash. But doing that would mean telling her how I've been considering all but cutting myself out of the family for his sake. Our relationship is strained enough as it is. I don't want it to snap because of a badly timed text. But before I can work out a reply, Sophie goes on.

Sophie: I'm sorry we didn't get to
say goodbye. Or talk about
everything that came up with Mom. I
didn't know you were having such a
hard time out there, Maddie. Just
know that I'm here for you, OK?

I smile sadly in my empty apartment. Despite her
hard edge, Sophie's always had a secret soft spot for
me and Anna. The three of us are like war buddies, in
a way—having gone through the trauma of our
father's death and our mother's collapse together.
Even though our battles are distinct, now that we're
adults, we'll always be rooting for each other from
our respective fronts.

Me: Thanks, Soph. We'll make it
through this somehow, I know it. I
love you.

Sophie: I love you too. Take care of
yourself.

The only way I know how to take care of myself at a
time like this is with a good, long session of girl talk,
some trashy takeout, and a bottle of something

fermented. And I think I know how I can get a hold of all three.

I pull up Allie's number from my contacts and wait for the healing to commence.

It's only by the grace of Allie that I make it through my first day without Cash. She races over to my apartment the second I tell her I'm home early, and that I need her. It's only when she arrives that I truly let myself fall to pieces. She's my best friend in the world, the only person who was there for me when I nearly dropped out of school, after my dad died. As I let loose the torrent of my conflicted pain, she doesn't even ask for details. I'll tell her what I can, in time. But for now, I just need a friend.

The coming week looms before me, daunting for its emptiness. I still have a week of vacation time left. My bosses aren't expecting me back until the following Monday. That means I have nothing to do for the next seven days but wallow in my own self-pity and loneliness…And that's just not something I can bear.

As hard as it is, I try to keep myself busy. I drive out to my favorite hiking spots outside the city, walking all day to drive thoughts of Cash from my mind. I tear through all my favorite books, willing them to sweep me away to worlds far away from my own. But some part of me always stays anchored in thinking of him—wondering if he's called, hoping that he hasn't written me off, and wishing that he'd show up under my window with a goddamn boom box like in the movies.

But as the days wear on, there's no sign of Cash Hawthorne. No calls, no texts, no sudden appearances. He wasn't kidding about the ball being in my court, now. If only I knew what my next play might be.

* * *

"Hey there, Mads! Long time no see."

I glance up from my office laptop with a tight smile for my boss, Brian (i.e. Mr. Intriguing). It's my first day back at ReImaged, but my brain still feels a million miles away. The only activity I've managed to do this morning is run endlessly through all the reasons I shouldn't care that I still haven't heard from Cash. It's been more than a week since we parted ways, and I've yet to hear a word. I keep telling myself that I've moved from despair to begrudging acceptance of our separation… Maybe if I think it enough times, it'll somehow become true.

"Hope you're feeling nice and rested after your trip," Brian goes on, rapping on my desk with his knuckles. He's in his mid-thirties, tall and lanky with an eager smile and a Silicon Valley bro's wardrobe. Brian's the good cop to his business partner Carol's bad cop, but I'm having a little trouble matching his enthusiasm this morning.

"Oh yeah. Montana was very relaxing," I tell him.

"Hmm. Montana," Brian says, nodding his head, "I never consider vacationing there. Very intriguing…"

Across the room, Allie glances up from her computer and cocks an eyebrow at me. I actually feel like smiling as Brian utters his buzzword for the first of many times today. Maybe this whole assimilating back into my real life thing won't be so impossible after all.

"Team meeting in five," says a no-nonsense voice from the doorway to the conference room. I look up to see Carol there, her eyes glued to her smart phone, as ever.

"Great," Brian smiles, "Allie, Maddie, we're gonna need 100% from both of you for this next campaign, so get ready to dive in."

"Oh. Maddie. You're back," Carol says, glancing up at me for half a second.

"Yep," I reply, "I just got back from—"

But she disappears from view without another word, completely blowing me off. A few years ago, I'd be miffed. But I've gotten pretty used to Carol's complete lack of people skills since I started working here. There's a reason Allie and I have the client-facing jobs at this business. You know—the jobs that actually require speaking with real humans.

As I start gathering my things for the meeting, I sneak another look at my cell phone. Still no messages from Cash—just an endless stream of passive aggressive texts from my mother. As per usual. Allie's hand closes around my wrist as I stare wistfully at the screen, and I look up bashfully at my redheaded partner in crime.

"Why don't you just text him first?" she asks me, "It's been a whole week, for Christ's sake. You have a right to know where you stand with him, Maddie."

I stuff my cell back into my desk drawer, a tiny twinge of guilt tugging at my conscience. Allie has been a saint all through my moping/moving on efforts. From the moment she showed up at my apartment that first Sunday with three kinds of Oreos, a gigantic bottle of Sauvignon Blanc, and a very absorbent shoulder to cry on, she's been my savior. I told her almost everything about the situation with Cash while we binge-watched about a season and a half of *Gilmore Girls*. Emphasis on the *almost*. I filled her in on every aspect of our relationship apart from the whole almost-kinda-related thing. I'm still wrapping my head around how I feel about that—I didn't want to spring it on her out of nowhere. I couldn't bear it if she thought my feelings for him were strange, perverted even. But *not* telling her is wearing on me, too.

"I don't want to make things any worse," I tell her, snapping my laptop shut. "Besides, I still need to figure out what I actually want."

"You want *him*," Allie replies bluntly, "That much is abundantly apparent. I don't see why you're not willing to give long distance a shot. Skype sex is actually kind of fun!"

"You never cease to amaze me, Miss McCain," I cut the conversation short as we set off for the conference room together. *God*. If only the single obstacle standing in my and Cash's way was a little distance.

Carol and Brian are already sitting at opposite heads of the conference table when Allie and I arrive. She and I will be tag-teaming this next campaign for Asphalt denim, an undertaking that totally slipped my mind while I was in Cash's orbit this past week. Another reason to keep my distance from him for the time being—I've got some serious work ahead of me. My job's been the most important thing in my life for years. It's baffling to have found something that even remotely challenges its hold on me. But then again, plenty of things about Cash baffle the hell out of me.

"OK!" Brian says, clapping his hands together as Allie and I sit down at the table, "Let's talk denim, ladies! This campaign is going to be a big one for us. We've never had a client in fashion before, and

Asphalt wants the full ReImaged treatment. If everything goes well, this will be quite the feather in both your caps."

"Well, you know how I love to accessorize," Allie smiles back at him. "I'll take an extra feather any day."

"Right," Carol says dryly, tapping a few keys on her laptop. At her command, a projection screen lowers down from the ceiling, a presentation about our next client all queued up. "Asphalt has been very specific about their needs for this campaign," she goes on. "We're going to help them plan several live events that underscore the more rugged side of their profile. Their new men's line is less high-fashion, more rough-and-tumble."

"So… Live hard rock bands, industrial spaces, partnering with some liquor companies…" I spitball, imagining possible angles for Asphalt's rebranding efforts.

"That's exactly right. Great instincts, Maddie," Brian says, bobbing his head, "As you know, the client's current reputation skews a bit elite. They want us to help bring them down to earth. Let the consumers know that 'real men rock Asphalt'."

"Oof. I hope that's not the final tagline," Carol winces.

"Real men, huh?" Allie echoes, her voice taking on a strange, agitated tone. She makes a show of tapping her fingertips on the table, playing at thinking hard. I know her well enough to know when she's up to something. "Why don't we lean into that angle?" she continues.

"Go on," Carol allows, sitting back in her leather chair.

"What if we could find ways to incorporate some brand ambassadors into the events? Maybe even some in the general marketing campaign if the client is into it," Allie goes on. "Asphalt is a west coast brand. What if we found local guys—small business owners, working men, cowboy types—to feature in the ad campaign for the new line?"

"Huh…Guys you could meet on the street, instead of professional models," Carol says, picking up on her wavelength.

"Or guys you could meet at a bar," she shoots back, a mischievous glint in her eye.

My stomach flips over as a grin spreads across my best friend's face.

"Uh. Yeah. I think I see where you're going with this…" I say, shooting her a look that clearly asks, *What the hell are you up to, lady?*

"I'm liking this direction," Brian says, "Very intriguing."

"How do you see this playing out in the Asphalt campaign?" Carol quizzes Allie.

"A lot of video content, mostly," Allie goes on without missing a beat, "We can produce short documentary-style spots of all the men we find, show them in their places of work wearing the new Asphalt line, have some interview footage where they talk about their super-manly jobs and whatnot. We can have the videos running all throughout the event spaces, give guests and investors something to interact with."

"So more atmospheric…I see…" Carol says, nodding slowly as she processes.

"What kind of man are we imagining here, exactly?" Brian piles on, hands clasped on the table, "Who can we use as a point of reference?"

"Actually," Allie replies, swinging her green eyes my way, "I think Maddie has a great lead on this one."

Brian and Carol turn to face me as I feel the color drain out of my face. What the hell kind of scheme does Allie have up her sleeve? Before I can diffuse the situation, Allie's made her way around to Carol's laptop and pulled up a new screen. I swallow a gasp as Cash Hawthorne's sculpted, wryly grinning face appears right there on the projection screen. A real, painful pang of longing twists my core at the sight of him, and for a long moment I'm rendered speechless.

"An acquaintance of yours?" Carol asks me, her own gaze lingering hard on Cash's gorgeous face.

"In a sense," I say faintly, shooting Allie a helpless look.

"This is Cash Hawthorne," my friend continues, "Maddie met him while she was in Montana. I pulled this photo from his business's website. He fixes motorcycles at a shop he owns near the state line. He's an Army vet, a tattoo and MMA enthusiast, and an outdoorsman. I think he could be *exactly* the kind of guy we're looking for, here."

"You forgot to mention the fact that he's sexy as hell," Carol says appreciatively.

You have no idea, I think to myself, blushing as the image of Cash standing in the altogether on the lake that morning of our sunrise fuck springs to mind.

"I say we move on nailing this guy down," Brian says, "He'd be perfect for this campaign. Tough, authentic, utterly intriguing. How soon can we make this happen?"

"Whoa, whoa…" I cut in, laying my hands on the table, "No need to be hasty, here. We can at least discuss some other candidates—"

"Why bother?" Carol says bluntly, "This Cash person is a great fit. We can't afford to dawdle here, Maddie. Asphalt has us on a tight deadline. You know this business is about creating a ballsy campaign, not a perfect one. Besides, Allie says you know this guy. We already have an in!"

Allie smiles at me across the table, shooting me a wink behind our bosses' back. I can't believe she managed to pull this off. More than that—I can't believe she'd go through all this trouble just to get me back on speaking terms with Cash. On the one hand, she's gone above and beyond best friend duty, here. On the other, she's also seriously crossed the line by taking the reins on this. She doesn't even know the full story, all the troubling complications, all the ways in which this relationship could ruin Cash and I both.

But I can't think about that now. Right now, my bosses are both looking at me expectantly, pleased as punch that I just happen to know the exact hunk they want to hire. I have no legitimate excuse not to follow through, no recourse to back down or pawn the campaign off on someone else. Allie's plan was flawless. I have no choice but to go with it.

"I guess you're right," I smile through gritted teeth, "Mr. Hawthorne would be an excellent fit for our campaign."

"I knew you'd think so," Allie replies across the table, folding her hands contentedly behind her back, "That's why I took the liberty of reaching out to see if he'd be available for a meeting this afternoon."

The conference room spins madly around me as panic and excitement battle for control of my mind and heart. Good god, this woman works fast.

"Love the initiative Allie," Brian says.

"Is he available, then?" Carol asks.

"He is," Allie replies, "He works long days at his bike shop, but he said he could take a few minutes to answer a couple of initial questions. He's expecting a representative from our agency later this afternoon."

"Is he local?" Brian asks.

"Not quite," Allie shrugs, "But he's worth the trip. We could just do a phone interview, but if you guys are already sold, I think a face-to-face meet would be preferable."

"Agreed," Carol says, "That's what you two excel at—face-to-face interaction. Maddie, you should take this first meeting, since you already know Mr. Hawthorne."

"Oh. But," I stammer, looking back and forth between my bosses, "Allie could totally take this one, too. She's the one who reached out, after all—"

"No, no," Carol cuts me off, "It should be you. Take the afternoon and pay a visit."

"But it's the middle of a workday," I protest weakly.

"Which is why I'm asking you to *work* on this assignment," Carol replies, out of patience with my pussyfooting. "What's the problem, Madeleine?"

"No problem," I rush to assure her, my heart hammering against my ribs, "I'll just…go and pay

Mr. Hawthorne a visit. See if he's interested in…working with us."

"Super," Brian smiles, clapping his hands together. "What a stroke of luck that you happened to run into this guy! How did you two meet, anyway?"

"He's…Uh…" I splutter, searching for the right words, "A friend of the family."

"Excellent, excellent," Brian goes on, nodding his head, "You know what they say, 'Keep it in the family!'"

I wrangle my face into a placid smile, despite the fact that I want nothing more in this moment than for a trap door to open up beneath my chair and swallow me whole.

"You can head out right away, Maddie," Carol tells me, "Allie, why don't you keep researching potential candidates? Brian and I will discuss some more logistics while you two get to work."

"Sounds good!" Allie chirps, walking around the table toward me. "Come on," she says, "We can chat on the way to your car."

I pull myself numbly to my feet, feeling as though I've stumbled into some alternate reality. My real life and the backwoods fantasy of last week are racing toward each other, set for a collision course. Will I even be able to handle these two separate parts of my life coming together? Or will I be leveled by the wreck their meeting is sure to cause?

"Allie, what the hell are you doing?" I hiss to my evil genius of a friend, the second we're out of earshot.

"At the moment, I'm walking you directly to your car to make sure you don't bolt," she replies smoothly, taking me by the elbow.

"You know what I mean," I shoot back, hurrying toward the front doors of the office. A little fresh air sounds pretty good right about now.

"Oh, you mean the whole 'making sure you don't blow it with the one guy you've actually cared for in years' thing?" Allie replies.

"Yes," I breathe, pushing open the front door and rushing out into the overcast afternoon, "That is exactly what I mean."

"Maddie, I admit that what I did back there was…unorthodox," my best friend allows, laying her hands on my shoulders. "But I couldn't just let you watch as your chance with this guy slipped away. I had to step in."

"You should have asked me," I reply, exasperated, "Or at least *warned* me. Now I have to drive halfway across the state and confront the man I've been pining away for—"

"Aha! You admit it!" Allie roars triumphantly, "You *have* been pining."

"I'm not—I didn't—" I stutter, "Goddammit, Allie. This isn't funny. This is my whole life you're interfering with, now. My career, my family—"

"What does your family have to do with it?" she cuts me off. "I thought your parents were friends? So what if it's a tiny bit awkward, they'll get over it. I still don't understand what the problem is."

"Let's just say there's….some history," I reply, averting my eyes.

"Well, fuck history," she says adamantly, taking me by the hand and leading me over to my car. "You can't change anything that's happened to you or your family, Maddie. You only have control over what happens right here, right now. You only get to make so many choices in your life. Usually, things are out of your hands, and you just have to take what you're given. But you have a choice with Cash, Maddie. You can choose to go get him, or choose to let him go. Now, I may have gone too far, getting in touch with him, but it's only because I can see how much you want him in your life. You can be mad at me all you like, but I won't let you spend the rest of your life being mad at yourself for fucking this up. I can't. I love you too much."

"Allie…" I breathe, resting my hands on the roof of my car in an attempt to steady myself, "How can I be sure that he'll even want me now?"

"You can't," she says gently, laying a hand on my back, "But you can at least be sure that you tried, this way."

"I know you're right," I whisper, "I *know*, but—"

"No more buts, Missy. You're on the clock," she says, pulling my car keys out of my purse and placing them firmly in my hand. "So go bag a stud, would you? We've got some denim to hock, and you've got a fuck buddy to get reacquainted with."

"I'm sure I'll thank you for this some day…" I say bemusedly, "Or else I'll never forgive you. It could go either way."

"You know what? I'll take my chances," she grins, "It's better than risking having another Paul on our hands. One more boring, lame ass boyfriend from you and I would have had to toss your ass anyway."

"Your confidence is ever-so-touching," I drawl, yanking open the drivers side door and sliding inside. "I'll let you know how this goes, I guess."

"Take your time," she tells me, turning toward the office, "True love and contract negotiations both happen in their own time."

"What a romantic," I mutter, starting the engine and peeling out of my parking space. Allie waves cheerfully from the front door, totally unaware of how high the stakes are for this little visit.

With my hands clamped firmly on the steering wheel, I turn the radio up full blast and set off once more toward Cash Hawthorne's turf. I guess I was bound to see him again one way or another…Our parents are cohabitating now, for god's sake. What's the real harm in speeding up our reunion? The real question is, what will he have to say when I arrive? Will he scoop me up in his arms and shower me with "I missed you's?" Or tell me to get back in my car and leave him the hell alone? At least I'll know one way or another before the day is out. That's one tiny shred of comfort in this otherwise bonkers situation.

I've barely made it onto the highway when the sprawling mid-day sky goes dark with storm clouds. Heat lightning crackles along the horizon, heralding a nasty downpour. Sure enough, the sky cracks open with a shattering peal of thunder. Buckets of rain slosh against my windshield—and I've got hours to go before I make it to my destination.

I wonder what Cash thinks about my impending drop-in? Does he think I'm totally pathetic, having had my best friend reach out to him instead of doing it myself? I can see how this stunt could come off as totally pathetic. I can't show up without knowing where his head is at. I reach into my purse, hunting for my phone so I can shoot him a preemptive text…but I can't seem to find it. My stomach sinks as I remember shoving my phone into at my desk drawer before the team meeting. I have no way of getting in touch with him before our surprise reunion.

"That's it," I mutter, pulling onto the shoulder of the highway as the menacing forces of nature tear at my beat-up car. I rest my forehead against the steering wheel, my mind reeling. I can't drive halfway across the state through a crazy thunderstorm for a man who hasn't even said he still wants me. A man I shouldn't even be with in the first place. I'm acting like a crazy person. A crazy, reckless person just looking for heartache. If I had even an ounce of sense, I'd turn around and head home right this second.

Just as I flip on my turn signal, preparing to make a U-turn, a twanging guitar riff sounds out from the speaker as a familiar, unmistakable voice croons…

"As sure as night is dark and day is light

I keep you on my mind both day and night

And happiness I've known proves that it's right

Because you're mine, I walk the line…"

My mouth falls open as Johnny Cash goes on singing about his will to "Walk the Line" for the person he loves. All at once, a wild, ringing laugh rips out of my throat.

"All right, universe," I crow, slapping at the steering wheel as amazed, excited tears well up in my eyes, "I get it. I think you may have just jumped the shark, but I get it."

Pulling carefully back onto the highway through the torrential downpour, I maintain my course for the small Washington town that Cash calls home. This visit could be a triumph or a disaster, but at least I'll always be able to say I threw caution to the wind…and all the other elements, too.

I won't come begging to your doorstep either, Cash Hawthorne, I think to myself, peering through the rain-splattered windshield, *But at least I'm gonna show up, for once.*

Chapter Eleven

I cut my headlights and force a deep breath into my lungs. Though the storm has let up some in the past few hours, the raging tumult in my heart has only grown wilder. This is the last remaining moment before I'm forced to make my final decision; the last chance I have to turn tail and run away as fast as I can.

But as bruised and baffled as my heart may be, it won't let me betray myself like that. Not after all this.

With trembling fingers, I cut the engine and sink back into the driver's seat, staring straight ahead at a modest brick building filled to the brim with motorcycles in various states of disrepair. And as I keep my eyes trained on the open door of the shop, a familiar figure strides into view.

My breath catches in my throat as I lay eyes on Cash. Though it's hardly been more than a week, my body rallies as though we've been apart for a decade. He's alone in the shop, working methodically on a bike as the rain pours down outside. His collar-skimming curls are even more distinct in the heavy summer air, falling across his forehead as he works. The muscles in his arms flex with each turn of his wrench, and every cell in my body remembers what it's like to be worked over by him.

But although I'm catching a glimpse of Cash in his element, the one place on earth where he should be most at peace, I can't help but notice the tightness of his jaw. The furrow in his brow. Something is troubling him, weighing down his mind even in this moment of solitude. It may be presumptuous—conceited, even—to imagine that he may be thinking of me. Of us. But if he's as wrecked by what's happened as I am, at least we can offer each other a spot of comfort, just by being face to face once again.

Before my rational mind can stop me, I push open the car door and step out into the downpour. I race across the lot, the warm summer rain soaking me in seconds. My heart beats out my marching orders, sending me flying toward Cash as fast as my feet can carry me.

"Cash!" I cry out, his name swelling inside of me, unable to be contained.

He looks up from his work, his hazel eyes blazing with recognition. I watch his mouth fall open as he rises, a look of amazement coming across his gorgeous face. I skid to a stop beneath the tin awning of the shop, my soaking wet body framed by the open door. For a long, silent moment, Cash and I stare at each other across the threshold, entranced by the sudden presence of the other.

"Maddie," he breathes, testing my name in the rain-scented air.

"H-hi," I stammer, a tentative smile playing across my lips, "It's so good to see—"

"How—What—" he says, taking a step toward me, "What are you doing here?"

My stomach flips over as he stares at me, clearly taken very much off guard by my sudden appearance. Now it's my turn to be confused. "I, uh…My job sent me," I reply, trying to jog his memory, "About the campaign? The interviews, or—"

"Wait," he cuts me off, cocking his head, "Just wait a second. You're here for work?"

"Yes," I tell him, trying to keep from quivering. I don't think it's just my wet clothes that have me shaking. It's the uncertainty about whether Cash is even happy to see me.

"That was *your* agency that called this morning?" he goes on, shoving a hand through his hair. "Why didn't you just…Why didn't you tell me you were coming?"

Did Allie conveniently fail to mention that I'd be the one arriving on Cash's doorstep this afternoon? Typical.

"It's a really long story," I breathe, steadying myself against the doorframe.

"Sounds it," Cash says, his expression unchanging. "But let me see if I've got the short version right. You're not here because you want to see me. You're here because you think I'd look good in a denim ad? Is that about the gist of it?"

"No!" I exclaim, hurt by his assumption. "You honestly think I'm just here for work?"

"What else?" he asks, crossing his arms, "It's not as though I've had any word from you, so how should I know?"

"I haven't heard from you either," I reply heatedly.

"Of fucking course not," he shoots back, "You made it pretty damn clear that what you wanted was time alone. To *think*. I may not be the brightest man around, but even I know what that means."

"Cash, please…" I murmur, bracing myself against the doorframe. "Just listen to me. I know I shouldn't have left you like that, without any explanation. Without any answers. But I did need to think. Because what I feel for you…it deserves to be thought through. It's too important to leave up to chance. We have to choose, Cash. If we want each other, then we have to choose each other. We owe ourselves that much."

He lets his eyes trail down along the length of my body, his inked chest rising and falling hard. My heart swells dangerously with hope. One harsh word from Cash, and I know it will shatter to pieces. When he speaks, his voice rakes along the bottom of his register in an impassioned growl.

"I chose you the first night we met," he tells me, bringing his searing hazel eyes to mine. "So. What do you say, Porter? Do you choose me, too?"

"Cash," I breathe, my knees going weak beneath me, "You…You must know the answer to that."

"I don't know a damn thing," he replies firmly, "Not anymore. I need an answer. Why are you here?"

My lips part as my brain reels through possible answers. I'm here because I don't know how to leave well enough alone. I'm here because I heard a song on the radio and thought I'd take my chances. I'm here because even though I know better, I still have a nasty habit of courting disaster, I guess.

But I know that no answer my mind can produce will be good enough for him, in the moment. He wants the truth. My truth. And that is something that only my heart can provide.

"I'm here…." I begin, my eyes stinging with sudden tears, "Because I need to be, Cash. Because I need to be…with you. I choose to be with you, if you'll have me."

He draws a deep breath into his lungs, drinking in my answer. I watch the truth wash over him, filling him with certainty.

"I was hoping you'd say something like that," he growls.

In two long paces, he's closed the space between us. He strides across the shop's threshold and enfolds me in his arms. I give my body over to him at once as he brings his mouth to mine. He spins me around, pushing me against the brick wall beside the shop's doorway. The taste of him as he kisses me harder and deeper than ever is like a revelation to me. I bury my fingers in his curls as he holds my face in his work-roughened hands, pinning me against the wall with his powerful hips. Rain courses down over the edge of the tin awning as thunder rattles overhead. But after a week of torment and heartache, I finally feel like I've reached the eye of the storm here in Cash's arms.

"I missed you so much," I gasp, as he pins my hands over my head, kissing along my throat with ardent need.

"You have no idea," he growls, as a low moan rises from my throat.

I can feel the raw, searing need for him coursing through my very blood as my heart pumps wildly. How could I have ever doubted my body's response to this man? This gorgeous, singular man? I arch my back as his kisses along my collarbone, pressing his lips to the soft rise of my breast.

"I hope you're the only one working here today," I breathe, grinning wickedly as rivulets of rain water course down my skin.

Cash raises his eyes to mine, fiery want smoldering there in his hazel-tinted gaze. In response, he grabs me by the hips and pulls me up into his arms. I wrap my legs around him, pressing my lips to his as my short pencil skirt bunches around my hips. Without another word, he carries me over the threshold of the shop, slamming the door behind us.

* * *

"How do I look?" I ask Cash, stepping back into the shop's private back office from the adjoined bathroom.

He turns around to face me, buckling his belt. His rippling, shirtless torso is still flushed from our vigorous reunion on the office's well-worn leather couch. A smile spreads across his face as he takes in the sight of me, standing before him in nothing but his white tee shirt and a pair of navy blue cotton panties.

"Very nice," he laughs, as I do a little spin for him, "It's a good look for you, Porter."

"Why thanks, Hawthorne," I reply, settling back down on the trusty leather couch, "It's nice, having something dry to wear."

"You were pretty eager to get out of those wet clothes in the first place," he teases me, sitting down and pulling me onto his lap.

"Excuse me," I laugh, "But I seem to recall that you were more than happy to get me out of them."

"I guess we're both a couple of sex fiends," he grins, circling his arms around my waist.

"Might as well accept ourselves for who we are," I sigh, brushing the curls away from his face. The stubble along his jaw is darker than I've ever seen it. As if he couldn't bring himself to be bothered with self care these past several days. The empty whiskey bottle sitting on his desk only fuels to my notion that he's been aching every bit as much as I have. But I get no satisfaction from knowing that we were joined in our misery. All I want is for him to be happy.

"Why do you look so concerned all of a sudden?" Cash asks, giving me a playful tug.

"I just feel so badly for how I left things," I murmur, "It was wrong of me to leave you back there at the house. There was just so much going on—"

"That's for fucking sure," he says, shaking his head, "But you're here now, aren't you? We don't need to drag all that shit back up."

"I'm sorry, is all," I tell him, "I need you to know that."

"Well. I'm sorry too," he says, "The ultimatums, the big talk…you didn't need that from me. Not after the bomb our parents dropped on us that night."

"Have you, uh…heard anything else? About their plans?" I ask him, tracing my fingertips absently across his chest.

"I left that place about two seconds after you did," Cash tells me, "Haven't heard a word since. Luke's back at Sheridan, now. And Finn's pissed off back to Portland, or so I hear. You never can tell with him. Good old Mom and Dad are on their own to fuck their shit up however they like, now."

"God. How did everything get to be so messy?" I ask, shaking my head.

"Maddie…we're out of there," Cash says softly, running his hands down my arms, "Let's just put it behind us. I like the view right in front of me much better."

"I can't just forget everything that happened at that house," I tell him, "Everything that's still happening between our families. Our parents. I mean, they're already moving in together. What if things go even further? What if they want to get married, or—"

"Slow down, would you?" he cuts me off, "First of all, take a breath. Nothing like that is going to happen, Maddie."

"How can you be so sure?" I ask him.

"Because there's no way my dad is going to get married again," he says simply, "That's the one thing I know to be true in this world. Hell, he's been driving it into my head since I was in the single digits that marrying my mom was the biggest mistake of his life. My brothers and I were raised to believe that monogamy and marriage are bullshit."

"That's encouraging," I scoff, raising an eyebrow.

"I said we were *raised* to believe that. Not that we actually do," Cash laughs, "Do I seem like a man who can be told what to think?"

"Not in the slightest," I reply, lowering myself to the couch next to him and curling up against his side. "I just wish I could put the whole thing out of my mind. Focus on this. On us."

"Why don't you try it?" he says, putting his arm around me. "Don't think of me as part of that whole Hawthorne-Porter shit show. Think of me as a sexy stranger you met in a bar. A sexy stranger you had your coworker track down like some kind of creep so you could get a little more tail…"

"That is *not* what happened," I laugh, giving him a little shove.

"Oh no?" he grins, "'Cause it sure seems like—"

"Allie tracked you down all on her own," I tell him, "And to be honest, she was acting more as my best friend than my coworker at the time."

"Ah. So the best friend already approves of me? I'm knocking this one out of the park," Cash says. "Does she know about our, uh, situation?"

"Not really," I admit, "I mean, I told her about that first night. She has photographic evidence, for god's sake."

"Ohh," Cash says, "She's the one who made the one night stand bet with you? Remind me to thank her when I meet her."

I sit up straight, looking at Cash with surprise.

"When you meet her?" I ask him.

"Well yeah," he says, settling back on the leather couch, "For this ad campaign or whatever the hell you're working on."

"You mean…you'd actually be interested in taking the Asphalt job?" I ask him incredulously, "For real?"

"Why not?" he shrugs, "You're gonna pay me, right?"

"Of course, but—"

"And from what your friend said, all I have to do is come to some parties and let you film me doing the job I'm already paid to do anyway?" he goes on.

"That's…the long and short of it, yeah," I smile slowly.

"Then I don't see why I wouldn't take it," he says simply, lacing his fingers behind his head. "This is my shop. It's not like I have to ask for permission. Besides, how could I deprive the good denim-buying people of America a look at this kisser of mine?"

"You know that most of the events will be in Seattle?" I ask him tentatively.

"How convenient," he says, "I'm pretty sure I've got a place to crash there."

I look away from him, shocked at this turn of events. I admit, I haven't had a chance to think past this afternoon. I figured I'd get to use this "interview" as an excuse to see Cash again. But past that…is it really a good idea to involve him in my work life? What if that added stress just brings this thing crashing down? A crease crops up between his eyebrows as I fall into silence.

"What is it?" he asks, cocking his head.

"I'm just. I wasn't—"

"Do you not want me to come or something?" he asks bluntly.

"What? No! I mean yes, I think," I blather, "It just never occurred to me that you *would*."

"You need to stop trying to figure out what I'm gonna do next," he laughs, standing up and striding toward the fridge across the office. "You'll be wrong nine times out of ten."

"Yeah, I'm starting to get that impression," I say, as Cash pops open the fridge and pulls out two bottles of beer.

"Let's say that I'm down to take this little job of yours," he goes on, opening the beers with his belt buckle. "What happens next?"

"Well…I was *supposed* to come here today solely to get a 'yes' from you," I laugh. "And your signature on the dotted line, of course."

"Guess you got a little more than you bargained for," he grins, handing me a beer, "No shame in that. You're a, uh…shrewd negotiator."

"Or something," I laugh, taking a swig of beer.

"So, you've got me on board," Cash goes on, "Now what?"

"Now…I guess you come to Seattle and meet the ReImaged team," I tell him. "That is, the people I work with…"

"You don't sound too excited about that," Cash observes, raising an eyebrow.

"It's not that," I rush to assure him, "I guess it just feels like asking for trouble. We already have plenty of baggage between us with our family situation."

"The way I see that, me coming to work for you could solve all that," he replies.

"How do you figure?"

"Because," he explains, "Working together would give us a whole new context of knowing each other. Our families wouldn't be our only connection anymore. We could just pretend we really did meet at a bar, and forget the rest ever happened."

"You mean…hide the fact that we're secretly almost-step-siblings from everyone we've ever met?" I ask, marveling at how ordinary this bizarre conversation feels.

"Pretty much," he shrugs.

"While also lying to our families by pretending we're not secretly screwing like rabbits?"

"Well, yeah."

I stare up at Cash across the room, my mind reeling. Do I really want to spend the foreseeable future leading some kind of crazy double life? Lying to everyone I know in some capacity? How can a healthy relationship possibly emerge from such a tangled web of deceit? Hell if I know. But sitting here alone with Cash, tucked away from the rest of the world, is the only thing that truly feels honest. So what if we have to lie for a while, in order to live our truth?

"So, what do you say?" he asks softly, "Think you can handle me crashing your real life?" I'm not sure if he's kidding or not.

"I have no idea," I tell him honestly, "But I thought you said I wasn't supposed to be thinking ahead?"

"You aren't," he winks, "It was a trick question. Good job, Porter. There may be hope for you yet."

"You're a real sonofabitch, you know that Cash?" I say, tucking my legs under me.

"Yeah, I've gotten that before," he shrugs, "But you know what that makes you?"

"Out of my goddamn mind for being crazy over you," I reply in all seriousness, taking in Cash in all his shirtless, beer slinging glory.

"That about covers it," he smiles, letting his eyes rake down my barely-clothed body. "You know...I don't think this storm is gonna let up any time soon, Maddie."

"Oh no?" I ask innocently, peering up at the rain-splattered office window.

"Nope," Cash sighs, striding across the room toward me, "That means I probably won't have any more customers today. I can close up shop right now. And I don't think you should be driving all the way back to Seattle tonight."

"It probably wouldn't be a very good idea," I agree, swinging my feet around to the floor. I let my knees fall ever-so-slightly apart as Cash approaches. "Do you know any place I might be able to stay tonight?"

"There is a motel over by my favorite roadside bar..." he grins, drawing to stop before me. "Maybe you know it?"

"Oh, I believe I'm intimately acquainted with that place," I smile up at him, taking another long sip of beer.

"Hmm..." Cash murmurs, trailing his fingertips down my bare leg. "Want me to jog your memory anyway?"

"Yes please," I breathe, as he sinks down onto his knees before me.

My head falls back against the black leather as Cash sets down his beer and places his cool hands on my thighs. Lowering his full lips to my skin, he kisses me just above the knee. Trailing his kisses slowly up my thigh, he pulls my hips forward, drawing me to the edge of the couch. That spot between my legs begins to throb as he presses my knees apart. Just moments ago, I thought that fervid desire was fully sated by our enthusiastic "hello again"...but I'm starting to realize that when it comes to Cash Hawthorne, I'll always have an appetite for more.

I hold my breath as he closes his teeth around the band of my panties, glancing devilishly up at me. He tugs the cotton garment with his mouth, easing it down over the rise of my ass, the slender lengths of my legs. Tossing my underwear aside, he turns his gaze to me. A low groan rises in his throat as I let my legs fall apart, opening even more of myself to him.

Looks like I'm not the only one who hasn't had their fill quite yet.

Without a word, Cash lowers his mouth to my aching slit. My back arches as I feel his warm breath against my wetness. My long, low moan rises above the sound of the rain pounding against the roof as Cash runs his tongue all along the length of me. His expert tongue strokes my pulsing, eager sex, sending shockwaves of pleasure up through my whole body. I gasp, grabbing hold of the sofa for dear life as he pushes back my flushed, pink flesh and exposes my raw, aching clit.

"Oh, *fuck*," I cry out, as he flicks that tender nub with the tip of his masterful tongue. "Oh my god, right there…"

"Oh, I know…" he growls, sliding two thick fingers inside of me as he traces quick, firm circles around that exposed button.

My cries erupt in the otherwise quiet room as Cash bears down on my clit with his exquisite mouth, thrusting his fingers deep inside me all the while. I can feel myself hurtling toward the heights of bliss, totally at the mercy of Cash's ardent attentions. I'm out of control, unable to form a single thought, a coherent plan of action. Now, as ever when I'm with Cash Hawthorne, I can stop overthinking—stop thinking at all—and be in the moment with him. And as he wraps his firm lips around my throbbing clit, sucks hard and fast enough to make me come like mad, I know there's not another moment I'd rather be living in.

As my body and mind come floating back down from the heights of bliss, I look down at Cash as he licks the taste of me from his lips.

"I have to say, Maddie…" he grins wickedly, "It's already been a pleasure doing business with you."

Chapter Twelve

The rest of my "work day" flies by in a rush of ardent lovemaking and shattering bliss. Cash closes up shop, and we have each other every which way before finally falling into a deep, satisfied sleep. His apartment takes up the second floor of the shop—a modest bachelor pad roughly the same size as my Seattle studio. We tumble into his bed just after midnight, spent from our day-long fuck fest of a reunion.

My eyes flutter open at the first sign of day, and I'm almost taken aback at how peaceful I feel—comfortable, warm, and safe. Cash and I are wrapped up in a well-worn quilt, totally naked, our limbs entwined. Could it really be possible to begin every morning this way? Could two people ever be so lucky?

Moving as little as possible so as not to disturb Cash, I reach down to where his phone is laying on the floor. Rolling onto my belly, I note the time. It's only five in the morning. I guess my body couldn't wait to get back up and at 'em…and by *'em*, I mean Cash, of course. It isn't until I note the date beneath the time displayed on the phone that it hits me.

It's Tuesday morning. I'm expected back at ReImaged at 10a.m.

"Oh for fuck's sake," I groan.

"Hmm? What?" Cash mutters, waking at once as he hears the distress my voice, "What's wrong, babe?"

I glance over at him, the gears of my mind spinning like mad. If we're going to set off on this next crazy adventure together, we may as well get a move on. There's not a moment to lose.

"How would you feel about a little road trip, Hawthorne?" I ask him, a mischievous grin spreading across my face.

After two very strong cups of coffee and a shower that only lets us indulge our dirty side one more time, Cash and I hit the road. I lead the way in my beat up car while Cash follows on his beloved bike. All along the way, I can't help stealing glances at him in my rearview mirror. With his leather jacket, sleek half-shell helmet, and dark jeans, he's every bit the prototypical bad boy biker. A real heartbreaker. But then why does my heart feel safer with him than ever before? Maybe I'm making a huge mistake, thinking I know the first thing about tangling with a man like Cash Hawthorne.

But it's too late to turn back now.

We swing by my favorite vintage shop in Seattle just after it opens, and I grab the first few articles of clothing I see. Can't show up to work wearing yesterday's clothes with a sexy stud in tow, can I? I shed my rain-washed clothes in the dressing room while the shopkeeper sees to me, eyebrows raised at the motorcycle-straddling hunk waiting for me outside.

"There must be a pretty good story there," the young woman observes, ringing me up.

"You have no idea," I mutter, smiling at Cash through the shop window.

Thus attired to appear like I haven't been fucking for the past 24 hours, I set off toward ReImaged with Cash trailing behind. Carol and Brian are going to be pretty pleased with this little surprise I'm bringing them. Hell, I'm pleased too, knowing there's a new place for Cash in my real life…even if that place is "eye candy" for my latest marketing endeavor.

Hey, it's better than nothing.

Cash and I stand side-by-side before the front doors of my agency, pausing to compose ourselves as best we can. He shoots me a sidelong glance, chuckling at how nervous I am.

"It's not like you're bringing me home to meet the parents," he points out, "That ship has already sailed, remember?"

"This is absolutely insane," I breathe, smoothing down my newly purchases yellow sundress. "Do you seriously think we can pull this stunt off?"

"If anyone can, it's us," he remarks, "And it's not like we don't have the motivation, right? The only question is, how am I going to keep my hands off you long enough to get through this meeting…?"

"You're terrible," I laugh, stepping quickly away from him as he reaches to give my ass a little squeeze.

"And *you're* blushing," he smiles, stepping up to the doors, "Get it together, Porter. This is a place of business."

In unison, we step through the front doors of ReImaged. At half past ten, the place is already buzzing with activity. A dozen employees mill about the open work space, collaborating and generating new ideas. Allie is sitting at her desk across from mine, already hard at work. But as her eyes flick up toward me and Cash, she goes absolutely still, openly gaping as we make our way across the room.

"Allie, I'd like you to meet Cash Hawthorne," I smile, more than tickled at her utterly baffled expression.

"Hey there," Cash says, extending his hand, "I hear we owe you one, Allie."

"Oh, it was…no trouble…" she says dreamily, shaking Cash's firm hand. Even with all her experience with men, Allie is still struck dumb by the sight of Cash, here in the flesh. And honestly, who wouldn't be?

"Why don't I go wash the open road off my face before I meet your bosses?" Cash suggests to me, looking around my office as if it were an alien planet. Something tells me this is the first time Cash has set foot anywhere that could be considered corporate.

"Bathroom's just through there," I tell him, pointing the way.

He tucks his helmet under a sturdy arm, nods at Allie, and leaves us alone at her desk. The second he's out of earshot, my best friend springs up out of her chair with an elated shriek and throws her arms around me.

"Who's your best friend in the entire world?" she grins excitedly, red curls quivering with vicarious excitement.

"You, and then some," I grin back, "I can't believe your little scheme worked out, but I've got to say…You're a genius."

"So you guys worked everything out?" she presses, her green eyes wide with glee.

"In a sense…" I tell her.

"What does that mean?" she asks, cocking her head.

"It means…Cash is going to take this job as a reason to be in Seattle for a while," I explain, "And we'll see how it goes."

"I'm sure that you're more than enough reason for him to come here," Allie points out, "But the job is a nice cover for you two."

"What do you mean, 'cover'?" I ask her, trying and failing to sound innocent.

"I mean, you two have a convenient excuse to do what you desperately wanted in the first place and make a go at being together," she replies. "So. You're welcome."

"Allie, I…actually have no idea what I would do without you," I tell her, in awe of her insight, "Seriously."

"You'd be having lackluster sex with Paul 2.0 and kicking yourself for not living a little," she shrugs, "No big mystery, Maddie."

Cash reappears, freshened up and gorgeous as ever. It's mind-blowing, seeing him here in this familiar place. But it's not jarring, like I expected. If anything, his being here makes me feel even more at home. Allie's right—it's like we needed some kind of permission to give into what we really wanted.

To her, it must seem incomprehensible that we'd need an excuse, being grown adults and all. But if she knew the underlying circumstances, I'm sure our hesitancy would make a lot more sense. To be perfectly honest, I still have to actively force the family-oriented worries from my mind. In the wake of my mom all but disbanding the Porter clan, I still can't shake the feeling that I'm betraying her somehow by sticking it out with Cash. I just hope that being a "bad daughter" in her eyes will get easier with practice. It's not as though I've ever been able to change her mind.

"Well, well…" Carol's husky voice rings out across the room. "Who do we have here?"

Allie, Cash and I look around to see the two founders of ReImaged heading our way. I smile gamely at Carol and Brian, playing it cool though my heart is pounding like a sledgehammer against brick.

"Carol, Brian, this is Mr. Hawthorne," I tell my bosses, "I hope you don't mind I invited him in this morning for a meeting. He was so enthusiastic to jump on board this campaign that I figured, why wait?"

"No reason I can think of," Carol goes on, her eyes glued to Cash's sculpted features. I've never seen anything ruffle my boss's feathers, but the very sight of my handsome new recruit has her gobsmacked. Even Brian, the straightest white dude anyone's ever met, stares at Cash with something approaching reverence.

"He's perfect," Brian breathes.

"He's ready to talk some terms, is what he is," Cash grins rakishly, tucking his hands into his jeans pockets.

"Of course, of course," Brian sputters, sweeping his arm toward the conference room. "Carol and I can walk you through the whole thing. It is such a pleasure to have you working on this. I find your whole story incredibly intriguing, I have to say…"

Cash cocks and eyebrow at me over his shoulder as Brian leads him off to the conference room. Allie moves to follow them, freshly printed contract in hand. Carol turns to me as they make their leave, admiration and excitement shining in her eyes.

"Excellent work, Maddie," she says, laying a hand on my shoulder. "I can't believe how quickly you were able to move on this."

"Thanks Carol," I smile, surprised by her praise. Approval isn't exactly something she regularly dispenses.

"He's the ideal centerpiece for this campaign," she goes on, eyes glued to Cash's retreating form. "Rugged, manly, no-nonsense…and sexy as the day is long."

"I'm inclined to agree with you," I allow, watching my boss straight-up ogle my lover's sculpted ass.

"I wish I'd known *he'd* be working for us someday before implementing that workplace sexual harassment policy," she sighs wistfully.

I fix my eyes on her, alarm bells clanging in my head. "What policy is that?" I ask, trying to sound casual.

"Maddie," she replies, crossing her arms, "This is a modern workplace. Brian and I made sure to write protections for all our employees into the company charter. Didn't you read the fine print in your contract?"

"Oh. Right. Of course. The fine print…" I reply, my voice strained. "But just to refresh my memory…?"

"We have a zero tolerance policy for office sexual harassment," Carol informs me, "And just to make sure there's no chance of any confusion cropping up, intra-office relationships are strictly forbidden. We've had to let more than a couple people go over the years for trying to pair off on the sly."

"…You don't say," I reply, feeling the color drain out of my face.

"Oh yeah," she nods, "You'd be amazed what people think they can get away with. But you know something, Maddie? The truth always comes out in the end. *Always*… Anyway! We've got Cash Hawthorne in the ReImaged web now. We should make sure there's no way for him to wiggle out, yes?"

I stare at her for a long moment, at a loss for words. But as usual, Carol can't spare a second to gage my reaction to her proclamation. She claps her hands together and sets off for the conference room, leaving me in the dust. I stand perfectly still as the chaotic office whirrs around me, rooted to the spot as the weight of this latest revelation comes crashing down on me. Just when Cash and I thought we were in the clear...

A surge of emotion rises inside of me, and I'm shocked to find a burst of laughter escaping my lips. I clasp a hand over my mouth, trying to contain a peal of giggles at the absurdity of this twist in events. Not a week ago, a blow like this may have sent me reeling. But now, after everything Cash and I have been through already, I can't even work myself up to being distressed. So we're officially forbidden from being together not only by the law, should our parents ever make their relationship binding, but also by our shared placed of work. The move that was supposed to solve all our problems has only doubled them. By rights, I should be freaking out.

But hey, what's one more insurmountable obstacle when you've got a man like Cash Hawthorne as a partner?

Pulling myself together, I square my shoulders and march off toward the conference room. Cash and I may not be the most traditional couple, or even an official couple at all, but lack of a title has no bearing on how devoted we are to each other. I'm always up for a good challenge, but I've never been as committed to seeing one through than I am right now. I have no idea what the future holds for the two us, or even whether that future will encompass a week or a lifetime. But I know that I'd risk everything to find out.

And if that isn't an act of love, I don't know what is.

THE END

...for now

Read below for an excerpt from the next book in the Stepbrother Bastard Series!

Join thousands of our readers *on the* **_exclusive Hearts mailing list_** *to receive FREE copies of our new books!*

CLICK HERE TO JOIN NOW

We will never spam you – Feel free to unsubscribe anytime!

Connect with Colleen Masters and other Hearts Collective authors online at:
http://www.Hearts-Collective.com, **_Facebook_**, **_Twitter_**.
To keep in touch and for information on new releases!

Also From Colleen Masters:

Stepbrother Billionaire by Colleen Masters

Stepbrother Untouchable by Colleen Masters

Damaged In-Law by Colleen Masters

Faster Harder (Take Me... #1) by Colleen Masters

Faster Deeper (Take Me... #2) by Colleen Masters

Faster Longer (Take Me... #3) by Colleen Masters

Faster Hotter (Take Me...#4) by Colleen Masters

Faster Dirtier (Take Me...#5) (A Team Ferrelli Novel) by Colleen Masters

Stepbrother Bastard (A Hawthorne Brothers Novel) (Book Two)

Prologue

The Bear Trap Bar
Montana, USA

Adrenaline spikes through my already boozy blood as I slam the bathroom door shut behind me. Flattening my back against the flimsy wooden barrier, I turn to face my unexpected companion for the evening. He towers above me in the dimly lit space, his sculpted features rendered all the more intense by the low light. His close cropped chestnut hair, dark stubble, and effortlessly cool style caught my eye from the very first second I saw him a few weeks ago. But in such tight quarters as these, every enticing aspect of him is amplified. The sheer pitch of my fascination with him renders me all but speechless as I drink in the sight of him, alone with me at last.

He's easily six feet tall, with a balanced, controlled body well conditioned by a lifetime of athletics and hard work. His cut, perfectly shaped muscles are rippling with barely contained desire. And as visceral as this moment is, it's still hard to believe that what he desires is *me*. God knows I've been fantasizing about finding myself alone with him for weeks on end. But now that we're here together, I'm almost overwhelmed by the hugeness of his want. The staggering, powerful presence of him. My breath catches in my throat as he plants his hands on the door above my shoulders, caging me in with mere inches of space between us.

"You sure you're up for this?" he growls, his dark green eyes smoldering in the dim light of the bar bathroom.

I draw myself up with a defiant stare, keeping my eyes trained on his face...no matter how overpoweringly gorgeous it is. Reaching around behind my back, I slide the door's heavy bolt into the locked position. The satisfying, metallic click rings out loud and clear in the small room, despite the cacophony of music and voices roaring in the bar proper. It's the last night of classes at the university nearby, where I'm just finishing off my junior year. Thank god I decided to ditch the frat-sponsored school-spirit shit show on campus in favor something a little more exciting. Or rather, *someone* a little more exciting.

"Does that answer your question?" I breathe, all but vibrating with anticipation.

He cocks a perfectly sculpted eyebrow at me, keeping me penned between his powerful arms.

"Not quite," he laughs, his voice ragged around the edges, "Try again."

"Wh-what?" I stammer, trying to keep up. At 21, I'm hardly inexperienced with the opposite sex. But even though this guy only has a few years on me, he's making the other men I've been with look like little boys. It's been a long time since I haven't been the more dominant partner in the bedroom…or, uh…bathroom, as it were. But where this particular man is concerned, I hardly mind. In fact, I actually find myself wanting to let him take the lead. And that is abso*lute*ly a first.

"I need a yes or no," he goes on, easing his perfectly balanced body toward me. My very cells are screaming to feel him against me. If he would just come a *little* closer…

"Would I have come back tonight if I didn't want this?" I point out, resisting the urge to throw myself into his thickly muscled arms.

"To be honest," he murmurs, eyes flicking down to my almost-quivering lips, "I'm having trouble getting a read on you. And let me tell you, that's not something I'm used to. You're gonna have to tell me outright what it is you want, here."

"Why don't you let me show you instead?" I shoot back, letting my hands trail down his rock-hard chest.

"Come on," he says, his full lips spreading into a rakish grin. "You already put it into writing, didn't you? What did that note of yours say again?"

"You're such an asshole," I mutter breathlessly, trying to fight the blush that rises in my cheeks.

"Oh, that's right…" he goes on, letting his torso brush deliciously against mine. He leans in close, his breath warm against my neck. Those firm lips brush against the shell of my ear, sending a shiver down my spine. "You want me to 'Nail you to the wall and fuck you dirty'. Wasn't that it?"

"That…Uh…That was the gist of it," I gasp, my thighs clenching together as a thundering rush of need courses through me.

"Say it then," he demands, brushing a lock of caramel blonde hair away from my face, "Tell me what it is you want, Sophia."

"I…I just…" I sputter, lowering my gold-flecked blue eyes.

"You'll tell me, won't you," he says firmly. It's not a question.

I force a deep breath into my lungs, gathering up every bit of courage at my disposal (liquid or otherwise). I'm not usually one for nerves, having conquered my stage fright at the ripe old age of four. Usually, that steadiness carries over into my romantic life…but not now. Not with him. For the first time, I don't feel like I'm *performing* desire, I'm *experiencing* it. Turns out, there's a pretty big difference—a difference so big that it almost frightens me. But if I've learned one thing from my life as a performer, it's that sometimes you've got to follow the fear if you want to find the truth.

"Luke," I start softly, my voice low in my chest, husky with lust.

"Yes?" he replies, his smoldering green eyes hard on my face.

I take his face in my hands, my fingers resting against his scruffy, razor sharp jaw, and lock my gaze onto his.

"I want you to nail me to the wall," I whisper, "And fuck me dirty."

A blaze of fiery need erupts in his emerald gaze as he takes me in. For just a second, he looks genuinely amazed that I've risen to the moment. I may have never had a man like him before, but maybe he's never had a woman like me either.

I let my lips part, a snarky jab at the ready to defuse the achingly intense moment. But before I can utter another syllable, he's pinned me to the wooden door with his powerful, tapered hips. A gasp escapes my throat as he snatches my hands from his face and holds my wrists firmly above my head. My entire body lights up like a flare as he brings his mouth to mine, kissing me hard and fast as he presses his incredible form against me.

My back arches as I open my mouth eagerly to his, letting his tongue sweep against mine. Our mouths move together, hungry and searching. I'm stretched out tautly before him, and he explores my dancer's figure with his firm free hand. My nipples go hard as he runs a hand slowly down my side, memorizing the lithe shape of me. He grins as he brushes a thumb over one of those erect peaks, pleased at how quickly he's turned me on.

"How long have you been waiting for this?" he growls, freeing my wrists as he kisses down along my throat. His lips leave sparks of sensation in their wake as they trail along my skin, and it's all I can do to keep putting one word in front of another.

"How long? Oh...Only since your very first class," I laugh breathlessly, writhing under his intoxicating touch.

"Hmm," he replies, grabbing me firmly by waist, "I've never met someone who was so turned on by personal finances. Kinda kinky..."

"It wasn't so much the subject matter as the it was the person delivering it," I smile, trying to catch my breath.

"That's good to know," he grins back, his voice straining with need, "It'd be a real shame if you just wanted me for my brain. The rest of me wants in on the action, too."

He shifts his hips ever-so-slightly, and I feel the hard, unbelievable length of him press firmly against my thigh.

My eyes go wide as I stare up at him, amazed by the enormity of his desire for me.

"Yeah…I get that," I breathe, letting my hands slide down his cut torso, "Though I have to say, I wouldn't mind getter a better…*feel* for it."

"Well Ms. Porter," he grins, as I whip open the buckle of his belt, "I'd be more than happy to give you one last lesson."

The din of the bar is entirely drowned out by the frantic pounding of my heart as Luke slips his hands up under my tank top.

"Go ahead, Prof," I whisper, "I'm a fast learner."

"My favorite kind," he growls back, as I slide my hand down the front of his blue jeans.

So consumed as we by our impromptu study session that we don't even notice as someone starts pounding on the bathroom door. We've got a lot of material to get through, after all. And I have the feeling that I've just discovered my new favorite subject: Lukas Hawthorne.

COMING SOON SUMMER 2015

Don't miss the release! **_CLICK HERE TO JOIN THE MAILILNG LIST NOW_**

43423371R00139

Made in the USA
Lexington, KY
29 July 2015